SUDDENLY HE WRAPPED A HAND AROUND HER UPPER arm and turned her to him. "What's wrong?" she asked, startled.

"Nothing. Everything."

His expression was sharper, grimmer, and more frustrated than it had been since she'd met him, she noted warily. "I don't understand."

"Don't feel bad, because neither do I."

He framed her face with strong, lean fingers. Gazing up into his eyes, she saw the glittering shards of a fiery ruthlessness. On her skin, she felt the blistering burn of his touch. She should break away from him, she thought, and run faster than she'd ever run before. But she waited, curious, mesmerized.

"This afternoon has been wonderful, Gabi."

"I've enjoyed it, too."

"I'm glad. But the thing is—it hasn't been nearly enough for me. I want more."

"More?"

"More time with you," he murmured, beginning to slowly lower his head toward her. "And much more of you."

WHAT ARE *LOVESWEPT* ROMANCES?

They are stories of true romance and touching emotion. We believe those two very important ingredients are constants in our highly sensual and very believable stories in the LOVE-SWEPT line. Our goal is to give you, the reader, stories of consistently high quality that may sometimes make you laugh, sometimes make you cry, but are always fresh and creative and contain many delightful surprises within their pages.

Most romance fans read an enormous number of books. Those they truly love, they keep. Others may be traded with friends and soon forgotten. We hope that each LOVESWEPT romance will be a treasure—a "keeper." We will always try to publish

LOVE STORIES YOU'LL NEVER FORGET
BY AUTHORS YOU'LL ALWAYS REMEMBER

The Editors

Loveswept® 814

The Damaron Mark: The Lion

FAYRENE PRESTON

BANTAM BOOKS
NEW YORK · TORONTO · LONDON · SYDNEY · AUCKLAND

THE DAMARON MARK: THE LION
A Bantam Book / December 1996

ISBN 0-553-44532-4

Published simultaneously in the United States and Canada

Bantam Books are published by Bantam Books, a division of Bantam Dou-
bleday Dell Publishing Group, Inc. Its trademark, consisting of the words
"Bantam Books" and the portrayal of a rooster, is Registered in U.S.
Patent and Trademark Office and in other countries. Marca Registrada.
Bantam Books, 1540 Broadway, New York, New York 10036.

PRINTED IN THE UNITED STATES OF AMERICA

OPM   0 9 8 7 6 5 4 3 2 1

ONE

A flat stretch of road opened up before him, the first flat stretch after miles of nothing but hills and curves. With a smile of satisfaction, Lion Damaron propped his elbow on the open window and pressed his foot down on the accelerator. The sleek, hungry car kicked forward, zoomed around the Jeep that had been in front of him, and then surged ahead.

It had been a long time since he'd opted to drive on a trip that involved any distance, but looking out on the Arkansas woods, bedecked in their brilliant fall colors of gold, orange, and red, he knew he'd made the right decision. There was a possibility that he had taken a wrong turn somewhere in the last fifteen miles, but he wasn't concerned. He'd get back on course soon enough. It was a Friday afternoon and he had the whole weekend before he was really due anywhere.

Crisp, cool air scented with pine whistled past

the window and whooshed into the car. The late-afternoon sun washed over the treetops, brightening the already vibrant colors of the leaves and making the air sparkle.

He slid a B. B. King CD into the player and turned up the volume. B. B. King, the open road, and a beautiful autumn afternoon. It didn't get any better than this.

Suddenly a rabbit darted across the road. He slammed on the brakes and instinctively swerved to miss the animal. The back end of the car fishtailed. He turned the steering wheel into the direction of the skid, but the car seemed to go airborne, and it flew off the road. A second later it hit the ground and began to plow its way down a slope through scrub and brush. Rocks pinged and thudded against it, branches cracked and scraped. Then with a light splash, the car came to an abrupt stop in a creek.

B. B. King blared incongruously.

Lion turned off the CD player and the ignition. Then there was only silence, punctuated by the loud pounding of his heart.

Driving about a half mile behind him, Gabi St. Armand witnessed everything and said a quick prayer that no one had been hurt. As soon as she reached the spot where she'd seen the car go off the road, she braked to a stop, jumped out, and hurried down the incline to see what she could do to help. Her heart was in her throat as the emergency procedures she knew flashed through her mind. She had left her cell phone at home, which meant she was simply going to have to deal with whatever problem she found by herself.

But before she could reach the car, its door opened, and a masculine figure unfolded from it. She slowed, then came to a halt. One look at the man and she was barely able to keep her mouth from falling open.

He was six-foot-two, maybe slightly taller, with a powerful build. His hair lay in expertly cut shaggy layers, its color shading from light to dark gold, with the single exception of a silver streak running from the corner of his right brow back through his hair. His skin was a burnished copper. His jaw was square, his mouth hard. Yet his lips were full and sensual and oddly beautiful.

She could have looked at them for a long time, but she forced herself to continue with her quick sweeping inspection. A heavy gold watch gleamed at his wrist. The crease in his brown slacks was sharp, the knitted material of his tan short-sleeved shirt was of the finest. His shoes, if she wasn't mistaken, were Italian, as was the fancy red car he drove. And the eyes he turned on her—she swallowed hard—were a riveting gold.

It was a good thing he wasn't going to need CPR, she thought with wry amusement. She probably wouldn't have been able to keep her mind on the procedure. "Are you all right? Are you hurt?"

"I'm okay." He grimaced. "Just a little shaken up, that's all."

"I'm very relieved. But your car . . ." The sympathy in her voice was genuine. It was a beautiful car.

"Yeah, I know." He turned to inspect it.

And while he did she continued to study him. And she came to the swift conclusion that he was the most devastatingly attractive man she had ever seen. He had the type of raw, powerful masculinity that, if a woman wasn't careful, could hit her between the eyes and stun her senseless. With his golden coloring and obvious strength, he reminded her of a lion who should be grazing the Serengeti Plains instead of standing in the piney woods of Arkansas, checking out the damage on his Italian sports car. Wherever he belonged, it wasn't here on this relatively lonely stretch of road.

In reality, he was too much for her senses to take in at one time. He was affecting every gland and pore in her body in ways she couldn't begin to define or understand. He was most definitely outside her experience—exotic, overtly sexual, vaguely predatory. There was only one way she could deal with him and help him, she decided. *She simply couldn't take the encounter with him seriously.*

Looking back at her, he thrust his hand through his hair. "Where did you come from?"

"You passed me a few miles back like I was standing still."

"The Jeep?"

"Right."

He remembered the car, but he hadn't paid any attention to its driver. Looking at her now, he was amazed at himself. How could he have been so fixated on the road that he'd missed her? She was lovely, *really* lovely, with sun-streaked, brown hair that brushed her shoulders and beige skin that appeared soft as velvet. She was wearing a denim jacket over a cream, scoop-necked T-shirt, a long, printed, cinnamon-colored skirt, and taupe suede lace-up work boots. And her large liquid brown eyes held real concern for him.

"Are you sure you're okay? I can take you to a hospital. Maybe I should anyway, just to double-check that you're truly all right."

"No, I'm fine. I'm just thankful there was no one else involved in the accident. I'm not sure what happened. A rabbit ran in front of me, but I should have been able to keep control." He glanced back at his car. Only its long front end was actually in the water, and fortunately the creek was shallow.

"You hit an oil slick."

His brows shot up in surprise. "An oil slick? I didn't see anything."

She grinned. "I'm not surprised. You were practically supersonic."

His lips twisted into a rueful smile. "Yeah, I suppose I was."

She laughed. "At the very least." She saw him tilt his head as if he were trying to hear more of her laughter, but she pushed the thought from her mind. He was an aberration, she told herself. He would disappear from her life as quickly as he had appeared.

He circled the back of the car to the other side for

a quick look. "The wheel base has been badly bent and there's probably a lot more damage that I can't see."

"There's no way you're going to be able to drive the car out of here."

He grimaced again. "Unfortunately, you're right. Listen, once you get into town, would you mind calling a garage for me?"

"I'll take you into town. There's an excellent garage there."

Faint surprise crossed his face. "Are you sure you don't mind?"

"Not at all. You need help, and lucky for you, I can do just that." He was probably from a big city, she reflected. In small towns, people rarely thought twice about helping someone in need.

"But you don't know me."

With a broad smile and perfect confidence, she held out her hand to him. "I'm Gabi."

After a moment's hesitation, he closed the distance between them and took it. "I'm Lion."

"Lion? What a perfect name for you."

She laughed, a shimmering sound that pealed through the air and the woods that surrounded them. He tilted his head once more, listening, frowning. Most women were somewhat self-conscious upon first meeting him, but she seemed completely at ease. In one way, her attitude was refreshing and charming. In another vague way, it was slightly irritating. "Lion is a family name."

"It's a wonderful name."

"Thank you, and thank you for your help. I'm very grateful to you."

"No problem at all. Do you have any luggage you need to get?"

"Yeah, I guess that would be a good idea."

She waited as he walked back to the car, bent in to retrieve his keys, then moved around to open the trunk. And she pondered his surprise at her offer of help. She'd have to be a half-wit not to know that he was a man who could definitely be dangerous to a woman. Not physically, though. No, he would endanger her composure, by disturbing and unsettling her. She knew this, because it had happened to her when she'd first seen him. But he wouldn't be able to rock her equilibrium again. She now understood perfectly that he didn't really belong here and that in a flash of an eye he would be gone.

He returned with a briefcase and a garment bag, both in a soft brown leather. "I'm ready."

"Great. Okay, come with me." She turned and headed off, throwing information over her shoulder as she went. "By the way, it looks as if you might need a bandage."

"Why?"

"You've got a couple of scrapes on your arm."

It was news to him, but he didn't bother to look. He was too absorbed with the graceful sway of her hips as she climbed back up the incline and the seductive swing of her glossy dark hair. Without another thought, he followed her. When he reached the road, she was waiting at her car, with a first-aid kit in her hands.

She opened the back door and gestured to the interior. "Sit and I'll take care of those cuts now."

"That's not necessary." He checked out the space behind the backseat and saw a large box taking up most of the room, so he placed his luggage on the floor and shoved it across to the opposite side.

With a smile, she tucked her hair behind one ear. "Maybe not, but humor me anyway. And while you're at it, thank your lucky stars. Things could have turned out so much differently, you know. If you'd been going any faster, you might have rolled the car or even smashed into a tree. Either way, I would have been calling an ambulance for you, instead of merely checking out a few scrapes. Which reminds me—I should have asked before—do you have a car phone?"

He'd been studying her smile and pondering how natural and comfortable she was with him, and it took him a moment to digest her question. "Uh, no. The car's new and I didn't have time to get one installed before I started out on this trip. I do have a cell phone, but I ran down the battery yesterday and never recharged it."

"And I left mine at home, but fortunately we don't really need them." She gestured again to the backseat. "Come on."

He shook his head. "No, really—"

"Oh, come on. Besides, I've carried this first-aid kit forever and I've never had an opportunity to use it. Who knows? I might have missed my calling to be a nurse, but I'll never be sure unless you let me see to your arm."

"Gabi, I wouldn't be able to live with myself if somehow I were responsible for you making a wrong career choice."

She laughed, clearly delighted with his answer. "I certainly do appreciate that."

He found her utterly irresistible, yet he realized she was treating him in the good-humored way one might treat a brother, a *younger* brother at that. He couldn't think of a reason in the world why it should bother him, but strangely it did. He slid into the car and settled back to watch her. She lay the first-aid kit on his lap and opened it. "According to the map, there's a little town not too far up the road."

"That's right." She tore open a packet containing an antiseptic pad and swabbed down the grazed area of his arm. "Gold Springs. My brother owns the garage there. It's the one I'm taking you to. We'll just run by there and give him the information on your car and then be on our way."

Her eyes were lowered as she concentrated on her task, giving him an excellent view of the lush thickness of her dark lashes. A lightly floral, lightly sensual scent rose from her skin. Her nails were short and bore only a clear coat of fingernail polish. She wore no engagement ring or wedding band or any other type of ring. The fact relieved him, he realized, and wondered why. With effort he brought his mind back to the business at hand. "It's going to take a special kind of tow truck."

"I'm sure he's got whatever will be needed."

She smiled and laughed easily, sweetly. Somehow he knew she would kiss the same way. "He's going to have to be careful. That car—"

"I know, I know—the car's worth a zillion dollars, at least. Don't worry, Rod's very, very good."

"Rod's your brother?"

"Uh-huh." She frowned over his arm.

He finally glanced down and saw a rather ragged cut. "I have no idea how that happened."

"It would be hard to say, but your window was open. Some branches could have scraped your arm as you were hurtling down the incline, but it's not at all bad. Not at all. You were lucky."

That was the second time she'd mentioned how lucky he had been, and he was beginning to believe it. But for an entirely different reason. "Gabi," he murmured.

"Ummm?" She rooted around in the first-aid kit.

"Is Gabi short for anything?"

"Gabriela. But only my mom and my grandmother call me that and then only sometimes. You know, like, *Gabriela, what have you done now?*"

"Do they say that often?"

"Quite often, actually. Let's see . . . for a bandage, I can offer you Day-Glo, Batman, or plain. What's your pleasure?"

"Plain will be fine."

She looked up at him, laughter glinting in her eyes. "Really? I'm surprised. I would have pegged you for a Day-Glo man, sure as anything."

"Why's that?" he asked, his normal husky tone even huskier. Her brown velvet eyes enticed a man to come closer, even when he knew an invitation was the last thing on her mind.

She gave a toss of her head, sending her hair in an arc away from her face. "Well, you're definitely not the plain kind, trust me. Here, we'll compromise. I'll give you a Batman one."

"That's a compromise?"

She nodded solemnly. "It's a nice in-between choice. It has a lot of character and it'll be a great conversation starter." As she was talking she smoothed it onto his arm.

"Whatever you say."

Something in his voice made her look up, and for a moment she was held by the fire she saw in the depths of his golden eyes. The fire was banked but nevertheless very hot. She snapped the first-aid kit shut and straightened away from him. "I say we need to get going. It will be much easier for Rod if he can get out here before dark."

"Fine."

"And then we'll get you checked into the hotel. My grandmother owns it. Her name is Margaret St. Armand."

"Wait a minute. Your brother owns the garage and your grandmother owns the hotel, and you just happened to be following me when I hit an oil slick that, by the way, I still haven't seen."

The sudden suspicion in his voice struck her as

funny. "What's wrong? Do you think I've got some kind of scam going?"

"Do you?"

"No, but now that you've given me the idea, I'll consider it for those times when things get slow."

"Does it ever get slow around you?"

"Sure." Still tickled by his notion about her running a scam, she stepped back and gestured. "Do you want to look at the oil slick?"

"Not particularly," he said, unable to take his gaze off her.

"Do you want to go to a different garage? A different hotel?"

"No."

"Well, good, then that's settled. Come on up to the front seat with me."

Dutifully he climbed out of the car, but before she could move away, a compulsion made him reach out and catch her arm. "Do you always boss people around this way?"

At the feel of his hand on her arm, her heart gave a hard thud. His touch had caught her off guard as much as his question had, but she quickly recovered. "Only people who crash their Italian sports cars into the creek, practically in front of me."

Releasing her, he grinned at her retort. "Well, I certainly fit that definition."

She searched his face, trying to gauge his mood. He seemed to be bothered by something about her, but she couldn't think what it could be. Perhaps the answer was as simple as the fact that he had been badly shaken by the crash. Anyone would have been. "Would you rather stay in the back?"

"Not if you're going to be in the front."

"Some people might scoff, but I've always found it easier to drive if I'm in the front seat."

His grin widened and her heart gave another thud, this time harder.

"Then I guess we'd both better move up there."

A minute later she was driving off and wondering why her heart still hadn't settled back to normal. But then she remembered the heat that had radiated off his body as he'd stood close to her and held her arm in his grip. He was truly the most magnetic man she'd ever met. It was a good thing she wasn't taking him seriously.

"So I'm going to be staying at your grandmother's hotel?"

The barbed humor in his voice made her grin ruefully. "I'm sorry. I've probably jumped the gun. You must have somewhere else you're scheduled to stay the night."

"No, not really."

She found that fact more interesting than she should have, she supposed. "No friends? Or business associates? No . . . uh . . . wife?"

"No."

She wasn't surprised to hear he was unattached. After all, it would be next to impossible to domesticate a lion. "Where were you headed? Do you have a schedule you're trying to keep?"

"No really set schedule. My goal for this trip,

other than to get some good driving in, was to check out some property north of here for the possibility of investment."

"You shouldn't be delayed too long."

"That's good, but I'm not really worried about it."

He leaned forward and with a pull of the lever moved his seat back to give himself more legroom, then shifted to get into a more comfortable position. And suddenly he seemed closer to her than he had before, though she knew it wasn't the case.

She'd been with him only minutes, but she already understood that he possessed far greater portions of virility and sexuality than most other men. "Where are you from? Texas? Your license plate is a Texas one."

"My home is in New York, but I flew to Dallas a few days ago on business. I finished early and thought I'd check out the property, but the decision to drive was a last-minute one." His lips twisted with wry humor. "To make a long story short, a friend of mine took me car shopping with him and I fell in love. I bought the car yesterday and started out early this morning."

She'd grown up with a brother who had been obsessed with cars all his life, so she understood about men and their toys. "Your car is only one day old? Oh, jeez, that's awful."

"It's no one's fault but my own. I was clearly enjoying myself way too much." He chuckled, and it dawned on him that despite the crash, he was *still* enjoying himself. Simply watching her and wondering what would make her laugh next would entertain him for hours on end—even though, so far, she seemed to laugh at *him* most often. She was definitely a new and unique experience for him.

The road began to climb and curve again, and the woods crept closer on both sides. He checked out her speed. "You seem to be driving every bit as fast as I was."

She threw him a relaxed smile. "The difference is, I know the road."

"Even the oil slicks?"

"No, but another difference is that *I'm* paying attention."

"*I* was paying attention."

"Uh-huh. To *what?*"

"To the day," he said, his tone dry. "And the colors of the leaves."

She laughed. "And the music. I heard your bass as you passed. It was pounding."

"B. B. King."

"You have good taste."

"I'm glad you approve." And amazingly he was. He tried to remember the last person he had wanted to please and couldn't think of even one person.

The curves began to come more and more frequently and the hills took them higher. Then they swung around one last curve, crossed a wooden bridge, and suddenly they were in Gold Springs.

At first glance it was a charming town, nestled at the base of the Ouachita Mountains with the glory of the fall foliage as a backdrop. At second glance, too, he quickly decided. The architecture ranged from Victorian to Art Deco, Greek Revival, and Gothic. Taking advantage of the crystal-clear day, local artisans were displaying their work on porches and in yards, everything from wood carvings to quilts, with signs that promised more.

Gabi looked over and noticed him studying the town. "Gold Springs use to be a booming resort town. People came from all over the world to 'take the waters,' as they use to say."

"What happened?"

"Pharmaceuticals mainly. After that, people no longer had to rely on simply the waters to cure their ills."

Some of the buildings and homes appeared rundown and faded, but many others looked freshly painted. And there was a nice stream of traffic. "The town looks as if it's doing pretty well."

She nodded. "It's coming back. People don't particularly care about the waters now, other than as a little mild curiosity. They come here for the laid-back way of life, the scenery, and the crafts, and the people who have lived here all their lives can make a decent living. It's nice all the way around." She turned into a gravel drive and drove up to a large, two-story, brick building with a sign above it proclaiming it to be ROD'S. "We're here."

The building looked like a home, and he eyed it curiously. "Where's the *garage* part of it?"

"Around at the back." With the completely natural way she had, she reached over and touched his arm. "Everything's going to be okay—you'll see. Come on, let's go find Rod."

Wonderful, he thought ruefully. Now she was re-assuring him. She had been nothing but kind, warm, friendly, and helpful toward him. And it was annoying the hell out of him. She could make his stomach knot simply by laughing. And her casual touch had him fighting an irrational urge to jerk her into his arms and kiss her until she was touching much more of him than just his arm. But even if he had wanted to turn the urge into action, he wouldn't have been able to. She was out of the car, across the drive, and inside the building before he knew it.

When he caught up with her, she was being hugged by a tall, slender man in workclothes, who had the same color hair as she did but darker eyes. Her brother, he assumed, and saw that she was laughing up at him. Of course she was, he thought, and was surprised to feel a surge of jealousy. Jealousy was yet another new and unique experience for him. It was also wildly inappropriate and totally aggravating.

Seeing him, she extricated herself from her brother's arms. "Lion, this is my brother, Rod."

Lion leaned forward to shake the man's hand. "Hello."

Rod returned the handshake. "Nice to meet you."

"Lion needs your help, Rod. About ten miles out of town, he hit an oil slick and flew, *literally*"—she tossed a grin his way—"off the road, crashed through the brush, and ended up in the creek. Luckily he wasn't hurt, but I'm afraid his car was. It's one of those low-slung Italian numbers. Gorgeous, even in the creek. You'll see for yourself—you'll be drooling, trust me."

The smile she gave her brother lingered on her face as she turned to Lion, obviously to see if he wanted to add anything. But the loving intimacy in her smile hit him squarely in the solar plexus, making it momentarily impossible for him to say anything.

"I can go pick the car up right now," Rod said quietly, his gaze on Lion. "No problem."

Gabi clapped her hands. "That's great. I told Lion you'd handle everything. And in the meantime I'm going to check him into the hotel."

He needed to say something, he told himself. Anything. "The car is an intricate, finely tuned—"

Gabi grasped his arm and pulled him toward the door. "He knows. Don't worry—your car will be in good hands. The best, in fact." She glanced back at her brother. "Give Angie and the kids my love and give Lion a call when you know the damage."

"Will do."

"Nice to have met you," Lion said hastily as he was hustled out the door.

"Sure thing," Rod called after him.

Lion barely managed to climb into the car and shut the door before Gabi started backing the car out of the driveway.

"Do you always move so fast?"

She spared him a glance as she pulled out onto the road. "Me? Fast?" Her surprise at his question quickly turned into amusement. "Hey, remember, *I'm* not the one who crashed."

"Right." He rarely drank anything harder than wine, but he suddenly found himself wishing for a good stiff drink of whiskey. "Rod didn't seem surprised to see you with a strange man in tow."

"Why should he be?"

"Does that mean you rescue men out on the highway on a regular basis?"

She looked over at him, merriment shimmering in her eyes. "Still think I might be running a scam, huh? No, no—it just means that Rod stopped being surprised by me a long time ago."

Was that even possible? he wondered. He didn't think so, certainly not in the short time he would have with her. "He also didn't seem daunted by the prospect of dealing with a foreign sports car."

"Your car will be fine, Lion. Honestly. Try to relax."

"I'm relaxed."

She looked at him and burst out laughing. "You're so funny."

He felt a peculiar lurch near his heart. Maybe he been knocked unconscious when his car had left the road, he mused, and he just didn't know it yet. Maybe she was in his dreams. But then again, no. He could have dreamed his entire life and never dreamed her up. If pressed, he wouldn't be able to say exactly why he found her so unique. He simply did. Perhaps a little more time with her would change his mind, but until then, he was finding her fresh and unexpected.

After several minutes of driving up and down hills, Gabi took a right onto a brick lane, which wound through more woods of oaks and hickory, their leaves aflame. The lane curved left, then right, then left again, and suddenly, unexpectedly, they drove into a clearing and Lion saw the hotel in front of him.

Six stories of Victorian fantasy, with one story layered atop the other in a slightly irregular, askew manner, the hotel was painted in creamy blues, yellows, and whites, with turrets here and there and gables everywhere. It looked like a beautiful frosted cake made with an impeccable touch of humor.

Delicately beaded spindle work extended around the entire wraparound porch, which was lined with tall-backed white wooden rocking chairs. A green lawn angled gently downward, and beyond it in the distance, he could see a lake sparkling in the afternoon sunlight.

"Welcome to the St. Armand," Gabi said, pulling the car to a stop on the circular brick drive. "The parking lot is around at the side"—she pointed to her left—"but I'll leave the car here for now."

"Do you want me to take care of that box in the back for you?"

"I'll have someone come out for it later. Thanks anyway."

She pushed open her door and slid out and he did the same.

Music and laughter greeted him as they drifted out from the hotel's open windows and flowed up from the group of men and women who were sitting in white wooden lawn chairs beneath a large spreading oak midway down the sloping lawn. "This is very nice."

"What did you think?" she asked, clearly amused. "That I was going to take you to a hotel straight out of *Psycho.*"

"The idea did cross my mind," he said, though it hadn't. Truthfully she had crowded out almost all other thought.

She laughed. "Sorry to disappoint you."

"I doubt very much if you could disappoint me," he drawled, then went still. He couldn't be certain, but he thought he'd seen something in her expression, a mere hint, really, that he had disconcerted her. But if he had, it had been brief, and in reality, it had probably been nothing more than a fleeting, odd shadow that he had misread. With a wry smile at himself, he retrieved his bags.

When he straightened and closed the car door, she gestured to the people sitting beneath the oak. "We have a group here this weekend for their twenty-fifth high-school reunion. They started arriving early today, and they're already having such a good time."

"A reunion? That must mean the hotel is close to full."

"Don't worry. We'll get you in, even if we have to put you in our broom closet." Grinning, she gestured toward the front door. "Come on. Let's go in."

It seemed to him as if he'd spent the entire afternoon following her and now he did it once again.

TWO

Just inside the lobby, Lion abruptly stopped, momentarily caught off guard by the almost magical and softly joyous mélange of color and warmth that was spread out before him. The lobby's large, airy space was filled with green plants and sunshine, and the same creamy blues, yellows, and whites of the hotel's exterior graced the interior's wood, fabric, and walls. But that was only the beginning.

Reds, oranges, golds, and greens dotted and swirled their way through florals, marched up and down the stripes, and dabbed at the squares. Sumptuously tufted chairs and deeply cushioned couches were done in velvets and damasks and hung with tassels and fringing. Occasional islands of fancifully patterned carpets floated over the gleaming oak floor.

To his right, a wide, arched doorway led into a big sitting room where the fantasy continued. And to his left, on the far side of the lobby, a long, gleaming mahogany desk acted as an anchor for the whole.

A fun, whimsical atmosphere had been created, he saw, yet somehow it had been kept perfectly true to the Victorian design of the hotel. But his awareness of his surroundings was short-lived as he realized Gabi, as usual, was walking well ahead of him. Before he could consider what he was about to do, he caught up to her, dropped his briefcase and garment bag, and grabbed hold of her arm. "Wait a minute."

Her hair whipped around as she turned quickly and looked up at him. "What's wrong?"

"How about your room?"

"What about my room?" Her tone was baffled.

As absurd and inconceivable as he knew it was, he wanted to shake her, physically *make* her pay attention to him. Even more absurd, he wanted to kiss her, learn her taste, figure her out. Because then *maybe*, after he'd gotten his fill of her, he would no longer be disturbed or unsettled by her. But none of those actions were acceptable and all were totally irrational. He settled for trying to shake her mentally as much as she was shaking him. "Do you live here?"

She nodded. "I have my own suite of rooms in the back beside my grandmother's. Why?"

"Because if there's no other room available, I'll bunk in with you."

Unbidden, uncontrolled, heat suffused her body. He'd only spoken of sharing her room, not her bed, but her mind went to work and her senses swam as she imagined musky scents, warm rumpled sheets, and the powerful feel of him thrusting deep inside her.

She pulled herself up short and attempted to clear her mind. She succeeded, almost completely. Almost . . . He was coming on to her, she told herself firmly. It meant nothing significant. She pulled her arm free of his grasp and strove for a light tone. "Don't fancy the idea of a broom closet, huh?"

"Not much."

Her pulses raced, but looking up at him, seeing his hard face and his glittering golden eyes, she came to the exact same conclusion she'd come to when she'd first seen him. It would never do to take him seriously, not even for a moment.

"Don't worry. I was just kidding. I'll find you a room."

He should have known he would fail to shake her up, he reflected sourly. He was beginning to doubt that she *could* be ruffled. She started off ahead of him, quick and beautiful, like a butterfly in flight. Perversely he pulled her back to him.

"What? What's wrong?"

"I'm not sure." He gave one more light, almost imperceptible tug and then her body was touching his. "I asked you this before, but you didn't give me a straight answer. Why are you always in such a constant hurry?"

"I seem like I'm in a hurry to you?" She hadn't been aware of hurrying, she reflected wryly. But if she had been, perhaps it was the age-old instinct of flight that always kicked in when a person was presented with danger. Either way, though, she was more than a little perplexed as to why it would bother him.

"Definitely. Do you always move fast, or are you just anxious to get me settled and off your hands?"

She had to make a conscious effort not to tense against the natural sexual energy he exuded. She understood what was happening, she reminded herself, and was therefore capable of handling it. She'd already accepted that he had been born with more than his share of virility and sexuality. Coming on to a woman would be as natural to him as breathing.

She gently extricated her arm from his grasp, then patted his shoulder. "Why on earth would you think I'd want to get you off my hands? I haven't been rude to you, have I?"

"You know you haven't." What she *had* done was manage to completely baffle him, something no one else had done, and the people he dealt with included some of the world's most powerful bad guys and captains of industry. Worse, he wasn't even sure he'd asked her the right question, so how could he expect to recognize the right answer?

She patted his shoulder again in a soothing manner he found irritating as hell, then took his hand and drew him along with her. "You're just upset, and rightly so. You've been through a lot this afternoon."

Now she was treating him like a child, he thought, something he couldn't and wouldn't tolerate, but before he could say anything else, he found himself in front of the mahogany reception desk.

"Hi, Gran," Gabi said, cheerfully greeting the

older woman behind the desk and at the same time releasing his hand. "I'm back."

"Well, so you are, darling."

The older woman possessed the same charming, mischievous smile as her granddaughter, Lion noted warily. Her short silver-gray hair softly framed a lovely face and her figure was slim and girlish. A heartbreaker in her younger years, no doubt, and in fact she probably still was.

She turned high-wattage hazel eyes on him, but she continued to speak to Gabi. "And aren't you clever? I sent you out for fifty pounds of flour and you came back with a handsome man. Well *done*, darling."

Gabi grinned at her grandmother. "The flour is in the back of the car, and this is Lion. He hit an oil slick and ran his new sports car into the creek. Rod's on his way right now to pull it out and assess the damage. Lion, this is Margaret St. Armand, my grandmother."

"Lion, call me Maggie." She held out her hand to him. "Nice Batman bandage, by the way. Not everyone could carry it off, but you do it beautifully."

A natural-born flirt, he thought with an appreciative grin as he shook her hand. "Thanks." After a quick glance at Gabi, he looked back at her grandmother. "You wouldn't happen to serve drinks in this fine establishment, would you?"

"Absolutely. I've always felt the ability to serve drinks was the very definition of a fine establishment. And our Pump Room serves everything from spring-water to whiskey. However, I must tell you that I'm reluctant to serve alcohol to a man wearing a Batman bandage."

"I *wanted* a plain one," he said with a grin and another glance in Gabi's direction.

"I tried to get him to consider Day-Glo," Gabi explained with perfect seriousness, "but he wouldn't have it."

Maggie shook her head, her expression distressed, the glint in her eyes pure mischief. "If you'd accepted the Day-Glo, I could have served you a Scotch, but as it is . . ."

The two of them were having a great deal of fun at his expense, he reflected wryly, and he could feel himself being pulled into whatever spell it was that they were weaving. "What can I do to make you change your mind about that whiskey?"

Maggie laughed with delight. "Honey, you already have. Handsome men are my downfall. I can't deny them anything."

"An admirable trait. By the way, I'm Lion Damaron."

Maggie gasped softly. "So *that* explains that very intriguing silver streak in your hair."

Gabi looked at his hair, then back at her grandmother. "What does?"

"The silver streak in his hair is called the Damaron Mark."

"Uh-huh. Okay. And it means *what*?"

"It means he's one of *the* Damarons."

Gabi looked at him blankly, trying to work out what her grandmother was telling her. "One of the . . . *Oh*. You're one of *the* Damarons." She paused as she assimilated the new information. "*Oh*. And that means you're *rich*."

She instantly regretted her rude outburst, but the fact that he might be rich honestly hadn't occurred to her before. Now she put his expensive sports car together with his expensively tailored clothes. The knowledge that he was a member of the well-known, extremely powerful family, with business interests around the world, only underscored the conclusion she'd already drawn. He was a man who belonged elsewhere.

Maggie smiled at him. "I'm afraid thinking before she talks is a concept she's always had trouble with. A weaker woman might have disowned her long ago, but *somehow* I've been able to bear up under the burden of being her grandmother."

Maggie was very easy to like, he reflected. "You're obviously a saint."

"I'm sorry," Gabi said. "I *really* am. It's just that I've never met anyone like you before, Lion." As explanations went, she knew hers was weak, but the man was having the strangest effect on her.

He looked at Maggie. "Do I really want to ask what she means?"

"Go for it," she said.

Gabi made another effort to explain. "Well, it's just that you're too much, Lion. I mean, *way* too much."

"I beg your pardon?" he asked, quiet, polite.

"You know," she said, certain that he did. "The

sum *total* of you. The whole package. I mean, what are the odds that you'd run into our creek? Zilch, I'd say." She nodded her head with relief, believing she'd finally been able to put what she was feeling into words. "You're simply way too much."

Maggie eyed her granddaughter thoughtfully. "That's a very interesting statement, darling. *Foolish*, but interesting."

"Well, it makes sense to me." Gabi shrugged, then moved to the computer behind the desk.

For the first time Maggie frowned. "What are you doing with that machine?"

"It's a computer, Gran—I keep telling you. And sooner or later you're going to have to learn how to use it."

"Nonsense. I have an excellent mind that requires neither software nor a computer repair tech, unless, of course, he happens to be good-looking." Maggie grinned at Lion.

As if her grandmother hadn't spoken, Gabi went on. "And what I'm doing is trying to find Lion a room." Concentrating on the screen, she typed fast. "I promised him he wouldn't have to sleep in our broom closet."

"Well, absolutely *not*," Maggie said, obviously shocked to her toes at the notion. "The day I waste a perfectly good man by putting him in a broom closet is the day I close the doors and retire."

Sensing support from Maggie, Lion decided to add something to the mix and see what happened. "I told her I'd be glad to share her room."

Light sparked in Maggie's eyes. "I *knew* I liked you. So what did she say?"

"She assured me she'd find me a room."

Shaking her head, Maggie tsked in regret. "She's dedicated to her work, so much so, she tends to get a little nearsighted at times."

"Perhaps a good optometrist could fix that problem."

"I was thinking more along the lines of a good man."

They both laughed.

Gabi's hands stilled on the keyboard. Just what she didn't need: her grandmother making a co-conspirator out of Lion. "Will you two stop talking about me as if I wasn't here?"

Maggie's expression was all innocence. "Of course you're here, darling. What on earth are you talking about? And by the way, our sixth-floor suite is vacant."

"I thought a couple from the reunion group had reserved that suite."

"They had, but one or both of them came down with the flu."

"That's too bad"—Gabi looked at Lion—"but it's your good luck. It's very nice, and it's nowhere near the broom closet."

"Sounds good, but how far is it from *your* room?"

She'd always considered herself to be very good-natured, she thought wryly, but Lion Damaron was really testing her. "*Too* far."

Maggie leaned toward him, her manner confidential. "I'll draw you a map."

He grinned. "Be careful, Maggie St. Armand. I just might fall in love with you."

She threw back her head and laughed. "There's no doubt about it—you absolutely will. Now why don't you go on up and settle in, then join Gabi and me for dinner."

"I'd like that, thank you."

Gabi quickly spoke up. "Uh, no—"

Whether by accident or design, her grandmother cut her off before she could get started.

"Robby?" Maggie looked around her. "*Robby?*" A young man of college age with thick blond hair and a ready grin appeared by her side. "Oh, good, there you are. Robby, this is Mr. Damaron. Would you please show him up to the sixth-floor suite?"

"Be glad to. Your bags, sir?"

He'd forgotten about his bags, Lion realized, and pointed to where he'd left them.

In moments, Robby had them in his hands and was back. "Follow me, Mr. Damaron."

"Sure thing." He glanced at Gabi. "I'm getting very good at following. See you at dinner."

Thirty minutes later Lion had showered and changed and was dialing his sister Yasmine's number. While he waited for her to answer he let his gaze wander around the unexpectedly elegant suite.

He saw muted, restful colors of cream, cocoa, and

burgundy, with accents of gold, and well-cared-for furniture of different styles. Fresh flowers mixed with autumn leaves filled a crystal vase. In the bedroom, fine linens covered the bed, and in the bathroom, amenities lined the ledge above the sink. There was even a lush terrycloth robe hanging on the back of the bathroom door, with *St. Armand's* embroidered on its breast pocket.

"Hello?"

He smiled at the soft sound of his sister's voice. "Hi, Yaz. It's me."

"Hey, big brother. Where are you?"

"I'm in the state of Arkansas in the town of Gold Springs, but I'm not really sure exactly where that is."

"Why not?"

With the phone in his hand, he strolled to the wide window and was rewarded with a view of a sweeping back lawn. A white Victorian-style gazebo that dripped with gingerbread graced one corner of the lawn. On another spot, croquet wickets were set up for a game, only needing the players. A badminton court was at another area. Pots and beds of flowers added even more color to the scene. Starting at the far edge of the lawn, woods provided even more glorious autumn colors. It all reminded him of another time, when things were slower and more gracious.

Except for Gabi, who was always in motion . . .

"Lion?"

"Yeah—well, it's like this. I bought a car in Dallas yesterday and started out this morning. I took a wrong turn, saw a rabbit, hit an oil slick that I have still never seen, ran off the road into a creek, and now I'm in a very nice suite in an amazing Victorian hotel in a place called Gold Springs."

"You had an *accident?*"

His lips quirked. Trust Yasmine to cut to the bottom line. "Yeah, but I'm not hurt."

"Thank *goodness.*"

"Yeah, and I was lucky in more ways than one. A girl was driving behind me. She's the one who brought me here."

"A girl?"

"A young woman. Her name's Gabi. She's . . ."

"She's what?"

"She's interesting."

"Really? I don't think I've ever heard you speak in quite that way about a woman."

"What way?" Suddenly his head jerked around and he scanned the room. "Wait a minute, Yaz. Hang on. I think I heard something." He couldn't see anything that might have made the sound, and he was sure the noise hadn't been a knock. He waited several more beats in case the sound was repeated, but it wasn't. "Okay, Yaz—sorry, I was mistaken. So what way?"

"I don't know, but there's something different about your tone. Tell me about her."

He grimaced, sorry now he'd brought Gabi up. What could he say about her? She confused and irritated the hell out of him, and at the same time made him want her, all without doing anything more than trying to help him. It made no sense at all. "She's always charging ahead of me."

"You mean she doesn't wait for you?"

"That's what I mean."

"Okay; well, that's interesting, I guess. What else?"

"She's always laughing, usually at me."

"Now that *is* interesting," she said, audibly muffling her own laugh.

"Yeah, and different." He strolled over to a table where he'd laid his briefcase and flipped up the top. "And annoying."

"Okay, give me all the information you have on her and I'll check her out for you."

With a computer and a modem, Yasmine could find out anything about anyone, and for a moment he was tempted. But an image of Gabi flashed into his mind, Gabi, with the sun in her hair and laughter on her face, lovely and guileless, her only crime that of stopping to help him. "No, don't do that."

"No?" she asked, surprised.

He understood. He wasn't acting normally, and at the moment he couldn't explain it. "No."

"Okay, then I won't."

"Good." He pulled some papers from his briefcase and tossed them on the table, then reached for the gold pocket watch that had been his father's and grandfather's. Checking the time, he found he had about ten minutes before he planned to go downstairs. "What are your plans for the weekend?"

"I'm going to Aunt Abigail's. Kylie is going to try

to break away from her studies and make it home. And Cale and Joanna are coming over on Sunday with my amazingly wonderful godson, Caleb Joseph Damaron Whitfield. I can't *wait* to see him."

"How is our newest little Damaron?"

"He's a Whitfield."

"That silver streak in his hair says he's also a Damaron."

She chuckled. "Yeah, it sure does. And Jo says he's doing great. In fact, the other day she held the phone up to him and he *talked* to me."

"Talk? Don't you mean he cooed and gurgled?"

"Yeah, but it was the most *intelligent* cooing and gurgling you've ever heard."

He laughed. "I believe you. Be sure and give everyone my love."

"I will." She paused. "I can tell something's bothering you, Lion. What's wrong?"

He ran his hand around the back of his neck and gave a self-conscious chuckle. "It's nothing serious."

"Okay. So what is it?"

"I don't know. Things just don't seem normal here."

"What do you mean?"

He thought about it for a moment, then shrugged. "It's just a feeling I can't put into words. Nothing for you to worry about." As he often did when he was thinking, he rubbed his thumb over the smooth gold case of the pocket watch. The idea that his father and grandfather had done the same thing before him helped him think and had comforted him during many a dark hour.

Suddenly his answer came to him. He was accustomed to calling the shots in all areas of his life. He spoke only once and his orders were instantly carried out. But from the moment he'd seen that rabbit, things had been out of his control. He felt much better, now that he'd finally figured out at least a *part* of what had been bothering him. "I wonder if that damn rabbit was white."

"White?"

"Yeah. I feel like I must have followed it down a rabbit hole, just like Alice."

She laughed. "Hey, I've got an idea. Why don't I fly down. I could be there by morning, or even sooner if you like. What do you say? Aunt Abigail will understand."

"No, no. I appreciate it, but it's not necessary. I'll be leaving tomorrow as soon as I get the news on my car."

"If it can be fixed that easily, then there must not be much damage."

"There's quite a bit of damage, but I can always rent or buy another car."

"You're sure you don't want me to fly down?"

"No, I'll see you in a few days. I basically just wanted to check in with you." And hear a familiar voice, one guaranteed to center him and bring him back to reality. "Do me a favor, Yaz, and give Wyatt this number. He may want to go over the info I sent out to him yesterday." He reeled off the hotel's number.

"Got it," she said. "Okay, see you in a few days. And listen, take care of yourself."

"You, too, honey. Bye."

As soon as the elevator doors parted, Lion spotted Gabi. She was standing behind the reception desk, talking on the phone. Maggie was also there, listening intently to what she was saying. He could see only a few other people, all involved with other things. It was a perfect opportunity to study Gabi, he concluded, and started toward her. An opportunity that he craved, he realized.

She had changed into a cream silk blouse with a V neckline that offered an enticing glimpse of her cleavage and discreetly caressed the delectable fullness of her breasts. As he drew closer he could see her jade-green skirt, which fell in graceful folds over the curve of her hips and down to her ankles. She'd discarded the lace-up work boots for a pair of low heels in a green that matched the skirt. Reaching the desk, he positioned himself near enough to overhear what was being said, but not close enough to be blatantly intrusive.

"I'm so sorry you haven't found your ring yet, Mrs. Griffin." Gabi rolled her eyes at her grandmother. "And I know you must have looked everywhere, right?"

"Ask her if she's thoroughly searched her suitcase," Maggie hissed.

"Uh-huh. And in all the pockets and folds of your suitcase? Uh-huh." She nodded at her grandmother. "Uh-huh. Yes, you did mention hearing strange noises, but as we told you at the time, this is an old hotel and it has a lot of creaks and groans."

Maggie tapped her fingers against the desk in an impatient tattoo.

"Okay, now, Mrs. Griffin, I don't want you to worry about a thing. We've contacted the sheriff, and we'll let you know as soon as we learn anything, anything at all." She nodded at something the woman on the other end of the line had said. "I will and you too. Thank you. We'll be talking to you soon." She hung up the phone and blew out a long breath. "You heard, Gran. She hasn't found it."

Maggie made a sound of disgust. "I'd bet money she misplaced it somewhere or just flat out lost it."

Lion moved closer and propped his arm on the reception desk. "What's up?"

Gabi looked over at him, apparently noticing him for the first time. "We've got a small problem."

Maggie gestured vaguely. "A former guest is saying that someone stole her ruby ring while she was here a few days ago."

He took in Gabi's worried expression, then returned his attention to Maggie. "But you don't think it was stolen?"

"Of *course* not. No one who works for me would steal. And none of our guests would either."

"Have you called Bo yet, Gran?"

Maggie sighed. "No."

"*Gran.* I *told* Mrs. Griffin that you *had.*"

"I know, I know, and I will." With a frown, Maggie absently patted the back of her hair.

Lion looked from one to the other. "What's a Bo?"

"Not what," Gabi said. "Who. He's our sheriff."

With an instant smile, Maggie nodded a greeting to a couple who were strolling by. When they had passed, the smile vanished as quickly as it had appeared. "I haven't wanted to call him, because I don't want him bothering my employees."

A grin finally broke out over Gabi's face, and the sight made Lion feel curiously better.

"She's very protective of her employees and guests, but what she's not telling you is that Bo is trying to court her and she's giving him a very hard time."

"The old coot," Maggie said.

Gabi chuckled. "He's not that much older than you, Gran."

"He's *still* an old coot. He's like a fox who suddenly decides he'd like the chicken he saw in the henhouse years ago, but what he doesn't have the sense to realize is that the hen is *long* gone."

Gabi bit her lip, clearly trying not to laugh. "You don't say."

"I do say." Maggie slapped her hand on the desk for emphasis. "But I guess I'll still call him. I really have no choice now. I was hoping that Mrs. Griffin would find the ring, but since she hasn't, I've got to make a report."

Lion's gaze rested on Gabi. Her laughter had faded and the worry had returned. "I suppose you've already checked the drainpipes in the room she was staying in."

"First thing," Maggie said, "and we found nothing. Look, you two go on in to dinner. I need to stay out here this evening."

"Why?" Gabi asked.

"Richard was suppose to be working the desk tonight, but he called in sick." She glanced at Lion. "His girlfriend, Mary Alice, needed attention is probably closer to the truth, but I don't really care. Richard is a good guy."

"You want me to stay and help you out?" Gabi asked.

"No, no." She sent her patented flirtatious smile Lion's way. "You can't leave a handsome man like Lion on his own for dinner. There's no telling what could happen to him. There are marauding savages everywhere and these days they wear lipstick and WonderBras."

Gabi's lips twisted wryly. "I think Lion is well able to take care of himself, Gran."

"That's what most men think, but they're wrong. Isn't that right, Lion?"

"I would never argue with you, Maggie."

"You hear that, sweetheart? He's not only handsome, but he's smart. All the more reason to go to dinner with him. Robby can spell me if it gets busy, but I don't think it will. Most of the guests are either dressing or already at their welcome cocktail party."

There were some arguments she could win, but Gabi knew this wasn't one of them. "All right, Gran. We'll go to dinner, but I want you to promise me you'll call Bo."

"For goodness' sake, Gabriela. Promise you, indeed. Anyone would think you don't trust me."

"Promise me, Gran."

"All *right*. Now *go.*"

For the first time that evening Gabi focused her full attention on Lion and received the strong, hot jolt of attraction that she had fully expected. The tweed sports jacket he wore was woven with browns, greens, and golds, and his shirt and slacks were both chocolate brown. It was a wonderful color combination for him, but the casual elegance of his clothes couldn't mask the power of his body, or hide the predatory nature she'd sensed in him from the beginning. And to her utter distress, her mouth actually watered. "Is this all right with you?"

A slow seductive smile curved his lips. "It's just fine."

She could handle him, she reminded herself. She *could*. She rounded the desk and gestured. "Then follow me."

Before she could get ahead of him, he reached out and took hold of her arm. "Since we're both going to the same place, why don't we walk together? That way we can get there at the same time. It'll be nice. Different. Civilized, even."

She couldn't help but laugh. "You're a funny man, Lion."

"So you tell me, Gabi. So you tell me."

THREE

She wasn't really surprised that her grandmother had opted out of the dinner she had set up, Gabi thought wryly, walking beside Lion. It was just like Maggie to arrange something and then duck out. She was a matchmaker from way back and subtlety had never been her strong point. In fact, she was sure Maggie had given Richard the night off.

For some time now her grandmother had been fretting about her. It didn't bother Maggie that her granddaughter wasn't married yet, nor did it bother her that she hadn't started a family. What did bother Maggie, though, and bothered her greatly, was that her granddaughter hadn't fallen in love yet.

There was one great love in every woman's life, her grandmother often said, and until she experienced it, she couldn't begin to really live her life.

She had dated often, Gabi mused. She'd even had

an affair, but, no, she'd never known true love. And so her grandmother continued to fret and plot.

What did surprise her, though, Gabi reflected, and surprised her greatly, was that Maggie had obviously decided that Lion was a prime candidate for her one great love. A strange choice, she thought, puzzled. Very strange, indeed.

First of all, she didn't *want* him. What woman in her right mind would? One look at him was all she'd needed to decide about him. He was a walking heartbreak waiting to happen. And one last, but very important fact about him was that he was going to be in her life *less* than twenty-four hours.

Experience the great love of her life in twenty-four hours? No, she didn't *think* so.

"Hi, Beverly," she said, greeting their hostess. Beverly was a very nice, middle-aged woman who had come to work at the hotel a dozen years ago to make extra money to help put her two daughters through college. But Beverly had come to like the work and the people so much, she'd stayed on, even though her daughters had long since graduated and were out on their own. "How's it going tonight?"

"Slow. All of our reunion people are at their party. We have Mr. Duncan, the Wentworths, and a few others—that's about it."

Gabi took in the large room with a quick, expert scan and realized she knew everyone there. Lawrence Duncan was a distinguished Englishman who was making a tour of America alone and had been staying at their hotel since the previous week. The Wentworths were a retired couple on vacation who had been guests of the hotel a few days longer than Lawrence Duncan. Local people, giving themselves a treat by eating out, made up the rest of the diners that evening.

Gabi turned back to Beverly in time to see a fawn-caught-in-the-headlights-expression frozen on her face—a product, no doubt, of noticing Lion for the first time. "I'm sorry. I should have introduced you two right away. Beverly, this is Lion Damaron. He's staying at the hotel for the night. Lion, this is our wonderful hostess, Beverly."

As the two exchanged greetings Gabi gave Beverly her silent sympathy. Over the years Beverly had seen a lot of men come through the restaurant's doors, but she obviously hadn't seen the likes of him before. She herself hadn't either, she thought wryly.

It wasn't that Lion was so good-looking, which in her opinion he was. Nor was it that he possessed such strength, which he obviously did. But his strength and good looks went beyond the mere physical, manifesting themselves in an innate self-confidence that riveted and compelled.

All in all, he was intensely male, intensely magnetic, intensely virile. And when he turned his golden-eyed gaze on a woman, he could make her go weak at the knees and the heart. *If* she allowed it.

"We're two for dinner tonight, Beverly. The corner table okay?"

"What?" Beverly tore her gaze away from Lion.

"Oh, sure. The corner table's just fine. I'll send over Ray."

"Great." Gabi automatically started off, but a few steps later she remembered that Lion seemed to like to walk *with* her and went back for him.

At the table, he pulled out the chair for her, but before she could sit, he bent his head to her and gave her a smile that practically curled her toes. "Nice," he murmured. "Very nice."

Her mind went blank. It felt as if her breath had backed up in her lungs. Thankfully, she managed to return his smile before her legs gave way and she dropped down into her seat. No, she definitely did not want this man. He was much too hard on her nervous system.

As he took the seat across from her, he did a quick survey of the intimately lit and refined ambience of the large, paneled room. "This is very pleasant."

Now that she had the security of the table between them she felt better. "So you were referring to the restaurant when you said nice?"

"You mean a minute ago?" A smile tugged at his lips. "No, I was referring to the fact that you came back for me. But *now* I'm talking about the restaurant."

She snapped the folds out of the napkin and laid it across her lap. "We try to please."

"You do an amazingly good job."

"Thank you." She had heard more than one meaning in his statement and silently chastised herself. There was no need to look for hidden intent. She doubted Lion would ever hesitate to say exactly what was on his mind. "By the way, did you ever get that whiskey you wanted?"

"No. Actually I forgot about it."

"You can order one now if you like."

He shook his head. "Wine with dinner will be fine."

"Okay."

"Have you always lived here in the area?" he asked, eyeing her thoughtfully.

"For most of my life. I went away for college, but after I was through, I decided to come back here and help Gran. I really love it here."

"What about your parents? Do they live here?"

"Yes, but they're in Europe right now. My dad is an architectural engineer and does consulting, so he can be away for extended periods of time. Whenever Mom and Dad had to be away when I was growing up, I always opted to stay here at the hotel with Gran."

"Sounds like you've had a nice life."

She'd never given the matter much thought, but he was right. "Yes. And you?"

Despite the subdued lighting, she saw something flicker in his eyes. "It's getting better all the time."

Her nerves jumped at the sudden, increased huskiness of his voice. Feeling so sensitive and touchy was new to her, and she planned to put an immediate halt to it. "You're a Damaron. You've got the whole world at your feet. I can't imagine your life has ever been that bad."

"Life has no respect for family trees, Gabi, no matter whose it is. In one way or another, the scales are always balanced."

She was involved in trying to interpret what he'd just said, but then he slowly smiled and she found herself caught by the sensuality of his lips and the heated gleam in his eyes.

"But it's *always* interesting," he added.

"Yes, it certainly is." When she had awakened this morning, she would never have guessed she would be having dinner with someone like Lion, someone who was so different from anyone she'd ever known, someone who was so incredibly fascinating. She looked over and saw Ray pouring coffee for another table, and knew he'd be at their table next. "I recommend the veal. Our cook has a really remarkable way with it."

Lion nodded. "Then the veal it will be."

"Just like that?"

"I've done everything you've said all afternoon, Gabi. Why should I stop now?"

For a moment it occurred to her to wonder just how far she could go with ordering him around, but then she had to smile at the ridiculous thought. He had done everything she had said because he had *chosen* to and for no other reason. If she knew nothing else about him, she knew that Lion Damaron was the type of man who would always do exactly as he wanted. "Then shall I order for us?"

"How about sharing what's behind that smile first?"

"Excuse me?"

"Your smile could give Mona Lisa a run for her money at being enigmatic, Gabi. What's so amusing to you?"

"Oh—just myself."

"That's a change. It's usually *me* you find funny."

She did, it was true. And she had the sudden, extremely inappropriate thought that she'd rather laugh *at* him than cry *about* him. "I mean no harm," she said, her tone gentle and sincere. "And I'm very sorry if I've been rude. It's just that a lot of things tend to strike me as funny."

"I can believe that."

Their waiter came up to the table, and Lion saw her eye him uncertainly. Slowly he grinned at her. "It's okay, Gabi. Go ahead and order for us."

"Okay, then," she said, and began to discuss their dinner with the waiter.

Lion sat back, but his gaze never once left her. He felt better this evening than he had this afternoon, he reflected. Much more in control. True, he'd definitely fallen down the rabbit hole and come out in a place totally different from what he was used to. But the place was charming and so were the people and he was having a good time. And he completely agreed with Gabi's earlier assessment of his situation: he'd been lucky and in more ways than one.

He waited until the waiter had left, then said, "You look very lovely tonight, Gabi."

"Thank you." She shouldn't be so pleased about the compliment, in spite of the fact that she had taken extra care as she'd dressed this evening. Still, she told herself, there'd been no harm done. There were many advantages to keeping a light, casual attitude toward Lion, one being that she felt free to tease him. With this in mind, she infused her grin with mischief. "You look quite lovely yourself, but then I'm pretty sure you look lovely all the time."

"Lovely?" One dark golden brow arched in a rather aristocratic manner. "You think I look *lovely?*"

"*Very.*"

"I've been called many things, but never lovely."

She chuckled. "Okay, okay, maybe I used the wrong word, but, Lion, I do think you're pretty amazing in a lot of ways."

His mouth quirked. "That's a compliment, right?"

"Absolutely. How can it be anything else?"

"Well, since it's you who is saying it—"

"Oh, come on, Lion, you have to give me that. You *are* amazing." She paused, trying to decide whether she should steer the conversation in another direction, away from any quicksand that might be ahead. But after several moments of contemplation, she decided that there was no reason to be coy with him. After all, she had no plans to go after him. "You're the sexiest man I've ever laid my eyes on. You're even fantastically rich. For goodness' sake, Lion, women look at you and *drool.* Surely you know that?"

"Is that a fact?"

His deep, husky drawl drifted across her skin, bringing heat and nerves to life. "It's a fact."

"*You* don't seem to be affected by me."

"Me?" She gestured and hoped it was as nonchalant as she'd tried to make it. "Oh, well, I'm different."

"You really are going to have to quit talking in understatements, Gabi."

"Understatements?"

"Never mind. Go on. So you don't drool when you see me?"

"Well, no, but normally I'm sure I would. You know, ordinarily. Well, what I really mean is—"

"Normally? Ordinarily?"

She sighed, regretting that she'd had the bad judgment to start this particular line of conversation. She rested her forearms on the edge of the table and leaned forward. "Look, I'm going to level with you, Lion."

"You mean you haven't been?" His mouth twisted wryly. "Just a minute—let me brace myself."

"I *have* leveled with you, but you're not listening to me."

"Trust me, Gabi. You have my entire attention."

She sat back again. "Okay, then listen to this, too. It's obvious that you're probably just about the best thing since sliced bread, but the truth is, I know better than to take you seriously."

No woman had ever even come close to saying the things to him that she was and he couldn't help but be a little thrown. And *more* than a little intrigued. "Care to explain what you mean by that?"

She held up a placating hand. "Maybe I phrased it wrong."

"By all means, try again. Maybe I'll like the new way better."

"Okay. I mean I can't take you as seriously as a woman might take a man in whom she's interested." She drew in a breath, then let it out. "See?"

"I don't like that explanation any better than I did the first one."

She eyed the movement in his jaw as a muscle flexed there. The conversation wasn't going exactly as she had wanted. "I'm sorry, Lion. I don't mean to hurt your feelings."

Hurt his feelings? He almost laughed. It was such a sweet, guileless thing for her to say. But it was also perfectly in character for her, he realized. She really *wouldn't* want to hurt his feelings. At the same time her candor was affecting him like a sledgehammer to his head and gut. She was extraordinary in every respect, including the completely unintentional way she made him want her.

She'd told him she wasn't interested in him, and everything she'd done or said reinforced that statement. So, why, then, did he find himself increasingly interested in her? And why did he keep imagining her on a bed beneath him as he made her completely his?

Determined to make him understand, she continued. "It's just that when I first saw you, you were so obviously out of place. I mean, there you were in an

Arkansas woods, driving an Italian car with Texas license plates and looking like you should be roaming the Serengeti. To top it all off, you and I wouldn't even have met if you hadn't run your car into the creek right in front of me. And then, of course, I learned that you're one of *the* Damarons, which means you can have anything you want and probably any woman too. And lastly, you'll be leaving just as soon as your car is fixed, or you buy or rent a new car, whichever comes first, and we'll never see each other again. So *why* in the world would I want to take you seriously?"

He stared at her. "That was quite a speech, Gabi."

She eyed him a bit warily. "But do you understand now?"

"To a point."

What else could she say? In reality, she didn't know Lion, and because she didn't, she was fully aware that she'd been commenting only on the *surface* of him. But his surface was overwhelming, and she had no desire to probe any deeper. "Please don't be hurt."

He smiled enigmatically. "You haven't hurt me, Gabi. Since we've met, you've bewildered me and you've irritated me and you've made me want you, but you haven't hurt me."

She'd been on a roll. She'd been sure she'd had everything under control. And then with one simple phrase—*want you*—he'd sent her reeling. She felt a warmth creep up her neck to her face. She had honestly believed his flirting and interest in her was more the reflex action of an extremely virile man than the fact that he really wanted her. She *still* did. Nothing else made sense to her.

She swallowed against a surprisingly hard lump in her throat that hadn't been there a minute ago. "Well, then, I'm glad that I haven't hurt you." She glanced around. "Oh, good, Ray. Thank you." As Ray placed their wine in front of them, she sat back and said a quick prayer of thanks for the diversion.

"Gabi?" came a soft, lovely voice. "I hope you don't mind if I interrupt you for a minute."

Her second prayer of thanks winged its way heavenward, though she noticed Lion didn't appear too pleased about the additional interruption. She smiled up at the couple who had stopped by their table. "Hi, Debra. Hi, Gordon. I'd like you all to meet a fellow guest, Lion. Lion, this is Debra and Gordon King. They're co-chairs for their reunion this weekend." She'd instinctively left off Lion's last name in order to afford him a measure of protection, even though she'd never known anyone who needed her protection less.

Debra and Gordon shook Lion's hand in turn, with Debra predictably staring a bit longer than strictly necessary at Lion.

"It's nice to meet you," Debra said.

Debra had been voted Most Beautiful of her high-school senior class, Gabi had learned when she'd looked through their yearbook. But in her opinion, age had made Debra even more beautiful, with her cream-colored skin and her shoulder-length pageboy.

Gordon, on the other hand, was pretty average in

height, weight, *and* looks. He was also developing a receding hairline. Reading the yearbook, she had learned he had been the football-team manager, along with being in the Spanish club. The two made an odd couple.

Gordon whipped out a business card and thrust it at Lion. "I'm in used cars. If you ever need a good used car and happen to be in Little Rock, come by and I'll fix you up with a real fine one. I'm the *King* of used cars. Get it? *King*. Gordon *King*?"

"I do get it and thank you. That's very nice of you."

Lion was the one being nice, Gabi reflected wryly, thinking of the outrageously expensive red sports car he had wrecked in the creek and his capacity to buy any car he wanted.

"Not now, Gordon," Debra said softly. "Gabi, I just wanted to tell you that everything's going very well so far."

"I'm so glad."

"I was also wondering if you had worked out the problem with the buses?"

Gabi nodded. "Yes, I did. I left a message for you earlier, but—"

"Oh, I'm sorry. We haven't been back to our room for several hours."

"No problem. I knew we'd hook up sooner or later. Three buses will be out in front in the morning at ten to take you all over to the high school." She looked at Lion. "Their high school is about thirty-five miles north of here."

"And so you're all going back to see it tomorrow?" he asked with polite interest.

"I'm afraid so." Gordon laughed, a bit too heartily. "We're returning to the scene of the crime."

"It's going to be fun." The softness of Debra's voice was in marked contrast to her husband's louder tone. "The high school is having an open house and lunch for us, and many of our old teachers will be there. Most of us haven't been back since we graduated."

"Most of us haven't wanted to." Gordon again laughed, but this time the laugh sounded blatantly false. "Up to now, we've been too smart for that." He glanced at his wife, saw the frown on her face, then shrugged. "But at least we'll have a football game to watch in the afternoon. Probably won't be any good, but—"

"It's the high school's homecoming game," Debra said in explanation to Lion. She took her husband's arm. "We'll be on our way so that you two can get back to your dinner. Gabi, thanks for sorting out the bus mess for me."

"I was glad to do it. Be sure and let me know if there's anything else I can do for you."

"Oh, there is one more thing. Has a Dr. Bill Douglas checked in?"

"No, but we're still expecting him. He's the only one of your group who hasn't registered yet."

Debra nodded. "He said he often has to deal with emergency walk-ins."

"Emergency." Gordon snorted. "Get a grip, Debra. He's a dentist, not a heart surgeon."

"Toothaches can be quite painful," Debra said, her pleasant demeanor firmly in place. She tugged on Gordon's arm. "Let's go, honey."

"See you all later, then. Lion, that's quite a ferocious name you've got there." As he and his wife made their way out of the restaurant, Gordon gave a booming laugh, as if he actually thought he'd said something original.

Lion turned back to her. "Quite an interesting couple."

"She's been very nice to work with."

"And him?"

"I mainly worked with Debra, so I haven't had the opportunity to get to know him, but I'm sure he's also nice. Oh, good, here's our dinner. Ray, everything looks just wonderful. Lion, I hope you like the veal."

"I'm sure I will." He leaned back in his chair, waiting while they were served, and studying Gabi the whole time as she chatted with Ray in her easy, happy way. When they were once again alone, he said, "I've been meaning to ask you something."

"Are you giving me a warning?"

"Not at all. I've just been wondering if, by any chance, you had something to do with the decorating of the lobby."

Her eyes widened in surprise. "Yes. How did you know?"

He grinned wryly. "It has the same joy as you do."

She pressed her hand over her heart. "Why, thank you, Lion. That's a wonderful compliment."

"You deserve it. You did a brilliant job."

"Well, thank you again. But I have to tell you it was fairly easy for me. The design and colors grew out of my knowledge and love of the hotel. And I had the absolutely best time ever doing it."

He nodded. "It shows. You have a real talent."

She shrugged. "I never thought about it as a talent."

"You should. And what about the reunion? Do you plan many events like it?"

"As many as come our way. It's so much fun to help people have a good time."

"You're obviously very good at it."

"I get a lot of pleasure from it." She picked up her fork, surveyed the food in front of her, and suddenly wondered why she didn't feel hungry. "I want to try to get in more groups. Even though we have quite a nice business with vacationers, groups would bring in new people who perhaps wouldn't have known about us any other way. Of course, the groups can't be too large, because we're a relatively small place, but other than that, we can compete with any of the hotel chains with our prices. And the St. Armand can certainly beat any hotel for charm and—"

"So you've labeled me as some sort of playboy without really getting to know me. Do you think that's fair, Gabi?"

Now she knew why she wasn't hungry. She'd been

dreading the moment when he would pick up their conversation where they'd left off.

"I never said you were a playboy. Besides, where on earth did you get that word? It's a bit outdated, don't you think?"

"Can you come up with a better word for the label you've given me?"

"I haven't *labeled* you."

"Oh, really? Then you tell me what you've done. Because it seems to me that you took one look at me and decided that, as you've said, you couldn't take me seriously. Come on, Gabi. You gave Gordon a better break than that. I repeat—do you honestly think you're being fair?"

He was right, she reflected ruefully. She wasn't being fair. And looking back to those stunning few moments after she'd first seen him, she had to admit the possibility that she'd based her decision about him on an innate need for self-defense. But even so, nothing she'd learned about him in the intervening time made her want to change her mind.

"Tell me something, Lion. Even if I *have* labeled you, why should you care?"

"Because I don't like people making snap judgments about me. And because I'd like to get to know you better, but you're making it impossible."

"We're having dinner together, aren't we? We're talking."

"I want more."

Of course he did, she thought wryly. Wanting more would be part of his nature. Tonight, sitting across a candlelit table from her, leisurely sipping his wine, he appeared almost domesticated. And there was a maddeningly attractive, sexy kind of laziness about everything he did and said. But complacency would be a mistake.

She put down her fork and rubbed her forehead. She'd tried very hard to explain to him how she felt, but he didn't seem to understand and she didn't know what else to say to him. It was all so clear to her, her stand so eminently practical to her. Even now, knowing what she did about him, she couldn't stop looking at him. If she felt an instinctive need for self-defense, it was no wonder.

He would be leaving. She would be staying. And when that happened, she'd like to be intact, her heart in one piece.

"What's wrong, Gabi?"

"Nothing. I just don't know why you're making such a big deal out of this. You're only going to be here a few more hours and then you're going to be gone."

He couldn't argue with her there, he reflected. In fact, he was amazed he was arguing with her at all. Minutes ago he'd told himself he was in control, now he wasn't so sure. She was getting under his skin—or maybe she was already there. "This is the twentieth century, Gabi. There are phones, faxes, planes. Just because we live in two different places doesn't mean we can't get to know each other."

She didn't buy it. To her, their meeting was similar to a shipboard encounter. It involved a relatively brief time, intense interest, and then the inevitable parting. In such cases, people usually had the very best of intentions and planned to keep in touch. But once they were back in their normal routine, life intervened and gradually they forgot.

She lifted her wineglass to her lips and sipped. "Do you like the veal?"

"I don't know. You might not have noticed, but I haven't eaten a bite."

"Then please." With a small wave of her wine glass, she indicated that he should eat.

"Changing the subject, Gabi?"

"Yes, I am. Frankly, I think we'll both enjoy our meal better that way."

Amusement lit his eyes. "Funny—I never would have taken you for a coward."

"I'm not a coward, I'm *hungry*. Look up the two words in a dictionary and you'll find they have two distinctly different meanings."

"Beautiful and smart make for an intriguing combination." With a grin, he picked up his fork and began to eat.

He probably meant smart *aleck*, and if he did, she'd have to agree. But as for the coward part—no. She *wasn't* a coward. She was sensible and practical, and she knew how to face the truth, which was exactly what she'd done in this instance.

A year from now, *if* Lion remembered her at all, he would remember her as only a blip in his life, a woman who had helped him one afternoon and dined with him that same evening. In fact, she'd probably end up being only one of hundreds of women with whom he'd dined.

She paused in her thoughts. *Hundreds* of women? Now she *was* being unfair to him. She had no basis for such a judgment except her own overactive imagination, and she had the ludicrous urge to apologize to him, even though she hadn't spoken her thoughts aloud.

She was making no sense, she thought suddenly. Not even to herself. And to substantiate that feeling, she realized a tiny part of her was beginning to dread the time when he would leave.

Lion was like a disruptive weather front that had blown into the middle of her calm life, but she had two things going for her: Weather fronts were always temporary. And while they were in the area, she knew enough to take shelter.

She looked up at him and saw his gaze fixed intently on her. "What?"

"I've been sitting here the last few minutes, trying to decipher all the different expressions that have been chasing across your face."

"And have you been successful?"

He nodded. "You bet. You've either been plotting a murder, or the overthrow of some government."

"Government?" She burst out laughing.

He slowly smiled. "It's been a while since you've laughed. I was beginning to suffer from withdrawal."

"Gabi does tend to have a strange effect on people, doesn't she?" Maggie said, strolling up to the table. "As I indicated before, she's always been a trial.

But what can I do?" She reached out to affectionately caress her granddaughter's hair. "From the moment she first opened her eyes and looked up at me, she captured my heart."

"I understand." His voice was soft, his gaze still on her.

Warmth curled through her stomach and pooled in her lower body, but Gabi did her best to *appear* composed.

"A man of true discernment," Maggie said with approval.

"What's up, Gran?" She wanted to divert the two of them before they started talking about her again as if she weren't there.

"Nothing, darling. I just wanted to check on you two. Lion, how are you enjoying the veal?"

"It's excellent."

"I'll tell our cook. He'll be thrilled."

"Please do."

"Gran, did you call Bo?"

"I said I would and I did. We made an appointment for tomorrow morning."

"Since when do you and Bo make appointments to see each other?"

"Since now. I'm glad I thought of it. What's more, I think it's an excellent precedent."

"Good luck on making *Bo* follow it." With a chuckle, she glanced at Lion and just managed to catch herself before she tumbled into the golden depths of his eyes. "I've got an idea, Gran. Why don't you sit down and finish my dinner? You haven't eaten yet and I need to check on the reunion cocktail party." As she spoke she stood and guided her grandmother to her vacated chair, neatly forestalling any objections.

"Well, thank you, darling," Maggie said. "This is very generous of you, but are you sure?"

"I thought you were hungry, Gabi," Lion said, his tone neutral.

"I was, but I've eaten enough, and I've just remembered that I need to make sure everything's running smoothly with the party."

"But, darling, you're not only giving up your dinner, you're giving up time with Lion too."

"I know, I know"—she congratulated herself on infusing a touch of regret into her voice—"but duty calls. I'll have Ray bring over more wine for you two."

Maggie turned twinkling eyes on Lion. "She's a bossy little thing, isn't she?"

"Oh, yeah."

Frowning, Gabi eyed the two. "You're doing it again, talking about me as if I'm not here."

"Well, you *are* leaving," Maggie pointed out with impeccable logic. "And I'll be delighted to finish your dinner. Your insanity is my gain."

"It's my gain too." Lion bestowed a dazzling smile on the older woman, then switched that same smile to her. "Gabi, will I see you later?"

"I'm sure I'll see you before you check out in the morning. Have a pleasant evening."

"We will," Maggie called after her as she turned and walked away.

Okay, she thought wryly, it was official. *Now* she was being a coward. And it was probably the wisest thing she'd done since she'd met Lion. This evening during dinner she'd discovered that no matter how determined she was to maintain a casual attitude toward him, she couldn't help but be affected by him.

She was attracted to him—truthfully she'd have to be dead not to be. But thankfully she still had the sense to know that nothing could develop between them. Her certainty on this went back to her belief that he didn't belong in her life. In fact, she had the eerie feeling that if she blinked the wrong way, he'd disappear right before her eyes.

She double-checked at the desk with Robby to see if there'd been any problems, then did a walk-through of the party and found everything going smoothly. As she was leaving she noticed Debra standing in a corner, deep in conversation with the Dr. Bill Douglas about whom she'd inquired. Gabi recognized him from her perusal of their yearbook. He'd been voted Most Handsome, and his looks had improved with age just as Debra's had. The two made a striking couple.

Glancing around, she discovered Gordon with a lively group of his classmates. Instead of sharing their laughter, though, he was glaring at his wife and Bill Douglas. Gabi felt a twinge of sympathy for him.

She'd almost made it to the door when she felt a tap on her shoulder and turned to find a stunning-looking woman with waist-length jet-black hair and almond-shaped eyes. "Yes? Can I help you?"

"No, but I can help you. Your aura is very disturbed."

"I beg your pardon?"

The woman gave her a knowing smile. "Actually, I'm the one who should be begging *your* pardon. I have a bad habit of speaking first and explaining later. But in your case, I honestly couldn't help myself. The aura of disturbance around you is so fierce and strong, I saw it from clear across the room."

"I see." Gabi searched her mind for an appropriate response, but in the end decided there was only one truly safe choice. "Well, thank you for telling me."

"I considered it my duty. And by the way, my name's Camilla. I'm here with the reunion."

Good, she thought. Now she was on familiar ground. "I'm Gabi St. Armand, and it's our pleasure to have you and your group with us." Despite her best effort, her professional spiel didn't deter Camilla one whit from what she obviously viewed as her mission.

Camilla fixed her with an earnest expression. "Listen, Gabi, you can triumph over this, it doesn't matter *what* it is or how *overwhelming*. All you have to do is *believe* that you can and you *will*. Okay?"

"That's good advice," Gabi said, bemused. "Thank you again."

Camilla nodded. "Anytime, and I do mean *any*time. I'll be here all weekend. Don't hesitate to call or come find me."

"I won't. Good night, Camilla."

Gabi pushed the strange encounter from her mind and spent the rest of the evening trying to keep from thinking about Lion Damaron and his departure in the morning. Eventually she gave up and went to her room, which was where her brother found her when he called.

"Wanted to let you know that I just talked with Lion."

"Really?" She quickly frowned. "So what makes you think I'd want to know?"

"You're the one who rescued him, right? And you're the one who took charge of his life this afternoon."

"Only because he needed help."

"Uh-huh."

"Did you say Lion was in his suite?"

"I didn't say, but that's where he was when I reached him a few minutes ago."

"Oh. Well, I was just wondering, that's all. The last time I saw him he was in the dining room with Gran."

"Then we know he had an entertaining evening, don't we?"

"There's no doubt about it. How long is it going to take to fix his car?"

"How long do you want it to take?"

"*Rod.*"

"I'm serious. I've got to order some parts, but there are several ways to do it—overnight express, the

regular ground rate, and then several choices in between. All you've got to do is tell me how long you
want him held up here."

The thing that astonished her was that she actually considered the choices, even though she knew
Rod was teasing her. "It doesn't matter which method
you choose and you know it. I'm positive you've already asked Lion what he wants."

"He wants it fixed as soon as possible, and if it
were my car, I would too. It's fantastic."

The excitement in her brother's voice drew a
smile from her. "I knew you'd fall in love with it."

"That and more. I may never recover."

She chuckled. "You're going to have to. You've got
kids to put through college."

He groaned. "Don't I know it."

"So what impression did you get from Lion? I
mean, did he give you the impression he might *wait*
for the car to be repaired?"

"He asked about a rental car."

She'd known he would, which was why she
couldn't understand the brief surge of feeling that
shot through her, a feeling perilously close to disap-
pointment. "Good, then he won't be delayed any
longer than he already has."

"Right. Listen, hon, I gotta go. Angie tells me it's
my turn to put the kids to bed."

"Give them a kiss from their aunt Gabi, okay?"

"Sure will. Talk to you soon."

She hung up the phone and glanced at her watch.
Normally she'd make one more round of the party

and the front desk, just to make sure everything was still going well, but she was tired, unusually so. Most nights she had to *make* herself go to bed. Tonight she suspected she'd fall asleep as soon as her head touched the pillow. Much as she hated to admit it, Lion's intensity had drained her more than she had anticipated.

Her hands went to the top buttons of her blouse just as the phone rang again. "Hello?"

"I just wanted to say thank you for everything you did to help me today."

She shivered, a strange reaction considering that a thick heat had entered her bloodstream the moment she'd heard the familiar huskiness of Lion's voice. "No thanks are necessary. I was glad to be able to help."

"I know you were, which is all the more reason why you deserve my thanks. There are a lot of people who would never have stopped."

"Well, then you're welcome."

"I also wanted to tell you how much I enjoyed our dinner together, brief though your part in it was."

Her hand tightened on the receiver—another strange reaction. "I enjoyed it too." She honestly had, despite her coward's retreat. "I understand Rod talked to you about your car."

"Yes. He'll be able to fix it, but it's going to take a while."

"But you plan to rent a car?"

"Rod gave me a couple of fairly local numbers."

"Good." An awkward silence fell between them,

and she found herself rushing to fill it. "Did you and Gran have a nice evening?"

"Yes, we did. Maggie is a remarkable woman." Amusement colored his voice. "She talked a lot about you."

Gabi silently groaned. "I'm sorry about that."

"Don't be. We had a great time."

"Told you all the family secrets, huh?"

He chuckled. "I don't know about that. But she did tell me about what a tomboy you were when you were growing up. She said you used to love climbing trees."

She grinned. "What can I say? I learned early the advantages of taking the high ground during a battle."

He laughed quietly. "Maggie did mention that you usually won all the battles you had with your brother."

"Looking back, I think it was mostly because he let me. Well"—she chuckled—"that *and* because I always had the high ground."

"If I promise to let you have the high ground—or rather the highest chair—would you meet me downstairs for a drink?"

She wanted to go. She didn't want to go. She changed her mind a hundred times in the span of a second. "No, thank you. I'm about to undress and go to bed."

"I'll be right there."

She recognized his teasing tone, but she also recognized that he was quite serious. She laughed to keep their exchange light. "I'm tired, Lion."

"I'm sorry to hear that, but in that case, have a good night and I'll see you in the morning."

"Good night."

She hung up the phone, already regretting her decision. One nightcap with Lion might be pleasant. . . .

She was reaching for the phone when she pulled herself up short. *What* in the world was she doing?

A nightcap with Lion might be pleasant *if* they could keep from arguing. And *if* he could keep from coming on to her. And *if* she could keep from reacting to the sexual heat he so effortlessly generated. But all that happened, plus *more*, each time they got together, so why was she even considering meeting him?

She rubbed her eyes with the heels of her hands, then ruefully shook her head at herself. She'd been totally certain that she had figured out what she needed to know about Lion, and exactly how she should react to him. But she now realized that, without her being aware of what was happening, she had started to take Lion seriously, *too* seriously.

It would never do. She had to stop and she had to stop now.

FOUR

Scents of pine and smoked ham drifted to Lion through the open windows of the sixth-floor suite as he sipped his coffee. He heard another faint burst of laughter and conversation and glanced at the time. It was nine A.M.

The reunion group was awake and ready for their next activity, even though many of them had stayed up quite late. Lion knew, because he'd also been awake through much of the night.

The sounds of their music and laughter had been welcome company for him, but about three or four, the sounds of their celebration had faded. And then, except for occasional odd noises and a glimpse of a raccoon scurrying across a lighted area of the lawn, he'd been left with his own thoughts.

He had managed to catch a few hours of sleep around dawn, more than enough for him. After waking, he'd showered and made a quick trip downstairs to fetch a tray loaded with a pot of coffee, a pile of freshly baked pastries, and a jar of the St. Armand homemade strawberry jam.

Now sipping the satisfyingly strong coffee, he noticed that the sun was already frolicking over the tree-tops and dancing across the grass, indicating another beautiful, crystal-clear day ahead. Driving should be as terrific as it had been yesterday, maybe even more so.

He glanced over at his garment bag, laid out on the bed, waiting to be packed. The phone number for the nearest rental-car business was on a pad by the telephone. It shouldn't take long to check out. With luck, he could be on the road inside an hour.

If he were leaving.

But he wasn't going to be leaving, at least not today.

He wasn't sure when he had made his decision. He wasn't even certain there *had* been a decision to make. More than likely, he'd known all along that he would be staying.

And why not?

He had the weekend free, a relatively rare occasion. The land he had been on his way to check out would still be there when and if he got around to it. Besides, he seldom took any real time off, and when he did, he was usually with family. And as long as he was taking time off, the St. Armand and Gold Springs appeared to be a perfect place to kick back and relax.

He really did need R&R. Some months ago he and his cousins had finally brought to justice the man who had been responsible for killing their parents. For many years the pursuit had taken up most of their time and effort. They had attended to their business interests, but anything personal had taken a backseat. It was how they had all wanted it. Now justice had been served, and they could get on with the rest of their lives.

"*Dammit*," he said loudly, throwing his nearly eaten croissant into the small wastebasket and slamming down his coffee cup. What in the hell was he doing, making excuses to himself? They were all true, but they were also all a smoke screen, intended to deceive himself.

Gabi was the reason he was staying, the *only* reason.

He had had women in his life, though none of them had ever become important enough or indispensable enough to make him think about a rest-of-his-life commitment. Or even to make him change a schedule that was only loosely set.

But yesterday, unexpectedly, Gabi had appeared in his life, offering help and laughter and a challenge. She saw him in strictly impersonal terms. To her, he was nothing more than a man whom she had briefly helped and who would soon be on his way out of her life. In the overall scheme of her life, she viewed him as no more important than any of the people who had gathered here this weekend for their high-school reunion.

To a certain extent, he could understand her

thinking, but it didn't stop him from being annoyed as hell.

He exhaled a long breath and rubbed the back of his neck. In reality, her effect on him was far greater than that of a simple annoyance or challenge. She intrigued him to the point that he had barely been able to sleep last night. He'd spent the major part of the long hours thinking about her and wanting her to the point of acute physical discomfort.

Desiring a woman had always been a relatively simple act for him, but desiring Gabi was proving to be extremely complicated. Because he didn't yet know the full extent of the complication, or have a handle on her or how he felt about her, he was going to stay one more day and try to get to know her better.

He glanced at his watch and decided there was no time like the present.

He spun on his heels and headed for the door. As he passed the table his gaze fell on his briefcase and he came to a sudden halt.

Gabi's head swiveled back and forth as she tried to keep up with the conversation between Maggie and Bo. She'd hoped to get them to take their discussion into the office, but Maggie had gone on the offensive the moment Bo had walked into the lobby. Thankfully, the last of the three buses carrying the reunion crowd had left, so there were no guests around.

"Look, Bo," Maggie said, her hands on her hips, "I don't actually want you to *do* anything. I only called you because I'm required to make a report so that Mrs. Griffin can collect on her insurance."

A large man with a broad chest, sandy hair, and the physique of a marine, which he once was, Bo towered over Maggie. He leaned down so that his eyes were level with hers. "*Doing* something is my job, Maggie."

Maggie lifted one hand from her hip and idly surveyed her nails. "You know I've often wondered exactly what your job is. It sometimes appears that all you do is visit with the best-looking widows and divorcees in this town."

He straightened. "Maggie St. Armand, you go around telling whoppers like that and your nose is going to start to grow, and let me tell you, a long nose is not going to be at *all* attractive."

"Oh, and I guess I only *thought* I saw you walking out of the florist the other day with flowers for Ida Mae Shugart?"

The laughter lines that perpetually crinkled at the corner of Bo's eyes deepened. "Ida Mae *Shugart?* Good grief, woman, where did you get an idea like that? Those flowers were for my *mother*. It was her birthday."

"Oh, sure, and I guess—"

"*Gran. Bo.*" Gabi hurried around the desk to them. "Please, go into the office where it's more private."

"Gabi's right, Maggie. You and I can argue anytime. Right now we need to talk about business, and the office would be the best place. I'm going to need a list of all your guests who were here during the same time as Mrs. Griffin, their names, their addresses, the dates of their stay. Oh, and do you have any guests who are still here from last week?"

"Yes, Mister—"

Maggie cut Gabi off. "Forget the office. *None* of my guests would have stolen that ring or anything else for that matter, so you can just forget that idea. I will *not* have you harassing them."

He slowly shook his head. "Maggie, honey, you've got to get over the idea that everyone who checks in here is your *personal* guest. I've told you that before. It will save you a lot of wear and tear on your nerves."

"And why *exactly* should I listen to you, now or ever?"

Gabi rolled her eyes and threw up her hands. She often found herself in the position of being a referee between her gran and Bo, and in every instance she had to admit that her efforts were useless. The two had known each other all their lives and were more than a match for each other.

"Why do you always have to be so gall-dang stubborn, Maggie?" Bo was saying. "It seems to me you'd use your common sense from time to time. Sure would be a nice change."

"Stubborn? You think I'm *stubborn* because I don't want you to accuse my guests of being thieves? Just let me tell you something—"

"You may have to change your mind, Maggie."

Hearing Lion, Gabi swung around. In the short time she'd known him, she'd seen many expressions on his face, but she'd never seen the grim expression he was wearing now. "Is something wrong, Lion?"

His golden gaze swept to her and rested for a moment. "Good morning, Gabi."

"Good morning. What's wrong? You look upset."

"Something of mine is missing."

His words accomplished what she had been unable to do: Make her grandmother and Bo focus on something or someone other than each other. They also sent an icy feeling of dread down her spine. *"Missing?* What?"

"My watch."

She automatically glanced at his wrist. "But you're wearing your watch."

"The one that's missing is a pocket watch."

Bo stepped forward. "I'm Sheriff Bo Carter. You're a guest here?"

With a nod, Lion shook the other man's hand. "Lion Damaron." He switched his gaze to Maggie. "I'm sorry to have to be the one to bring you such bad news."

Maggie clasped her hands in front of her, so tightly the skin gradually turned red. It was something she did only when she was extremely worried, Gabi reflected.

"Don't be silly, Lion," Maggie told him. "I'm the one who's sorry. Goodness, I don't even know what to say. It's just so hard for me to believe—" She paused and for a fleeting moment her expression turned hopeful. "Is there *any* way you could be mistaken?"

"Believe me, I wish I was, but no, the watch is gone. It was in my briefcase and now it's not."

"And you searched the room? It couldn't have fallen under the table or into the wastebasket? Or maybe even under the bed?"

Gabi felt so sorry for her grandmother. The idea that someone was stealing in her hotel was very hard for her to accept. She just wished she could think of something to do or say to make it better for her.

Lion shook his head, his lips tight with regret. "I did make a cursory search, but I'm never careless with this particular watch. I had it out for a few minutes yesterday, but I'm positive I returned it to my briefcase and now it's not there."

Bo whipped out a small black notebook and a pen. "So when exactly did you last see it?"

"Last night."

Bo began to write. "And I assume you've been out of your room since that time?"

"That's correct. I was out of the suite for some time last night, and then I left the suite this morning to come down for coffee."

Maggie's face was pale, her hands still tightly clenched. "This simply has to be some mistake. Nothing like this has ever happened here."

Bo glanced over at her, taking in her lack of color, then put his big arm around her and pulled her to him. "I'm sorry, honey. But don't worry. We'll get it all figured out for you. I promise."

Gabi wondered if her grandmother realized just how naturally and easily she had gone into Bo's arms.

She had accepted his offer of comfort without question. But no matter how distressed she was, her spirits were rarely dampened for long.

"I do *not* want my guests disturbed, Bo."

He gave her a quick hug. "I told you not to worry. I'll be very discreet."

Maggie pulled away. "Bo Carter, you're about as discreet as a bull in a china shop."

Good humor spread over his rugged face. "I've never broken a single piece of your china, Maggie St. Armand, and I don't plan to start now. You're just going to have to trust me."

"Trust you?" Apparently the concept was so novel to Maggie, she momentarily ran out of words.

Bo took advantage of her silence. "For now I'm going to assume that the two thefts are tied together. That means I won't have to talk to the folks that are here this weekend for the reunion, because they weren't here at the same time as Mrs. Griffin. I'm going to start off by talking to your employees, along with any guest that's been here since last week." He looked at Gabi. "I gather there are some."

Reluctantly she nodded.

Bo turned to Lion. "Mr. Damaron, if you don't mind, I'd like to talk to you now. I'm going to need a detailed description of the watch and a couple of more facts."

Lion nodded. "Certainly. And please call me Lion." He looked at Maggie, then at Gabi, and his gaze lingered. "You're going to have me on your hands a little while longer."

"*What?*" Gabi couldn't keep the surprise from her voice.

The news immediately perked up Maggie. "That's *wonderful*, Lion. I was really hoping you wouldn't be leaving us just yet."

"You're *staying*?" Gabi couldn't get her mind to accept the news. She had been so certain he would be leaving today, so certain he would be going out of her life. It had taken a bit of doing, but sometime during the night she'd finally been able to restore her perspective on Lion—the impact he'd made on her life in the short time she'd known him, the fact that she couldn't allow him to affect her any further, and the fact that he would be leaving. But now . . .

He smiled at her. "I'm staying. I hope there's no problem with that."

"Oh, of course not. No, not at all."

"What about the suite? Is it free for the rest of the weekend?"

Maggie spoke up. "It's all yours for as long as you want it. The fact that you're staying is a great example of something good coming out of something bad. I'm feeling much better about the whole thing."

Lion bestowed a dazzling smile on Maggie. "I'm glad. Sheriff? Shall we go up to my suite?"

Bo nodded. "That'll be great. Maggie, while I'm upstairs with Lion, would you please get together your employee records for me?"

"No." She folded her arms beneath her breasts and glared up at him. "You're going to have to look someplace else for your thief. No one who works for me would steal."

His smile was gentle and understanding. "Uh-huh. Well, then if that's the case, they've got nothing to worry about, now do they? Get me those records. Lion"—he gestured—"after you."

"That man is positively insufferable," Maggie muttered, watching the two men walk away.

"Which man?" Gabi asked, her gaze on Lion's retreating back. To her chagrin, she discovered that the graceful, deceptively easy way he moved was almost hypnotic.

"*Bo*, of course. If he thinks he can come into my home and my business and boss me around, he'd better think again."

Gabi looked at her. "It's his job, Gran. And you better cooperate with him, because the sooner he finds out who's taking things, the better off you *and* your guests are going to be."

Maggie muttered something that Gabi didn't bother to try to figure out. Her mind was already on another subject. "The problem is . . ."

"The problem is what?"

She hesitated, then decided to save herself some time and her grandmother an interrogation by coming clean right off the bat. "Lion. The problem is Lion."

Maggie's face cleared. "Honey, that man isn't a problem, he's a downright *miracle*."

"But why in the world would he want to stay, Gran? What does he care about one watch? He must have a drawerful, not to mention the ability to buy another—in fact, as many as he wants."

Maggie stared at her with an open mouth. "That cannot *possibly* be a serious question, Gabriela."

"Serious?" Her brow knitted. "Of course it's serious."

"My poor, poor baby—you can't see what's right in front of you. Lion is staying because of *you.*"

"Oh, for heaven sakes, Gran, be realistic."

"I'm being perfectly realistic. *You're* the one who's having trouble with the concept of realism. And let me tell you, I do not understand that *or* your attitude toward him. If I were your age, I'd be on that man like honey on Winnie the Pooh's nose."

Gabi couldn't help but laugh. "I don't think I even want to imagine that particular scenario."

"Ah-*hah*! That's your problem—no *vision.* For heaven sakes, Gabriela, snap out of it. If you would just give Lion a tiny bit of encouragement, you could do much more than *imagine.*"

With a sigh, she pinched the bridge of her nose with her thumb and forefinger. "Okay, Gran, try to follow me on this. It's an ordinary day, with ordinary clouds in the sky, and ordinary chores to be done. You walk out to your backyard, and lo and behold, you see Kevin Costner standing there."

"Kevin Costner?"

"That's right. Kevin Costner. Now, you *know* he doesn't belong there. You *know* he's got a whole other life somewhere else. And you *know* that if he's there in your backyard, it's because he's lost or something, and that pretty soon he'll be on his way again. You see? Well, that's exactly how I feel about Lion Damaron. So *now* do you understand?"

"No."

"No?"

"Kevin Costner doesn't do a thing for me."

Gabi's eyes narrowed on her grandmother. "Uh-huh, okay, then how about this: Ordinary day, ordinary clouds, et cetera, et cetera. You go out to your backyard and you find *Sean Connery* there."

With a sudden moan of ecstasy, Maggie clutched at her heart. "Oh, my word. If that ever happened, you'd have to bury me the next day, because I'd just curl up and die of sheer happiness."

"Then you understand."

A wicked gleam of mischief lit Maggie's eyes. "Honey, I said you'd have to bury me the *next* day. But that leaves one whole day, and you can bet I'd never let Sean Connery out of my backyard until I'd used and abused him and in the process probably given us both a heart attack."

Gabi gave a shout of laughter. "*Gran.*"

"Don't be so shocked. *You're* the one who put Sean Connery in my backyard."

She threw up her hands. "I give up."

"Good. Now go find Lion. And don't forget to give him some encouragement. I have a really strong feeling that he could turn out to be the love of your life."

A warm, sweet breeze flowed through the lobby and the sitting room. The curtains languidly billowed. As the minutes of the afternoon ticked by, a soft light slowly advanced across the oak floors, and a serene quiet filled the hotel, except for the occasional muted sound of a hammer or saw from work being done on a far back section of the building.

Gabi drew in a deep, contented breath. She was happy, she realized with a start of surprise.

Truthfully, she was usually happy, but she hadn't expected to be in such a good mood this afternoon. At this moment Bo was in the office with Gran, going over the employee records. The mere thought that there might be a thief among them was enough to make her cry.

But there was also something else going on. At this minute, instead of being on the road, putting distance between himself and the hotel, Lion was out on the front porch in one of their wooden rocking chairs, reading their local newspaper.

She gave absolutely *no* credence to Gran's idea that he was the love of her life, nor did she consider even *one* of Gran's outrageous suggestions. But she *was* happy that Lion was going to be staying. Go figure, she thought with a smile to herself as she moved from behind the reception desk and headed toward the open front door.

Lion looked around as she strolled out onto the porch. "Hi."

"Hi, yourself." Her smile broadened in an immediate reaction to the sight of him. He looked so comfortable, leaning back in the rocker, the ankle of one leg resting atop the knee of the other. He wore a golden-brown shirt, open at his throat, and the long sleeves folded back to reveal muscled forearms. The shirt was tucked into another pair of impeccably tailored tan slacks. "You look very peaceful." And quite wonderful, she added to herself.

"It's a very peaceful place. Do you have time to sit for a while?"

"Sure." She'd come out for the express purpose of talking to him. She sank into an adjacent chair, adjusted her long patchwork cotton skirt over her ankle boots, then leaned back and sent the chair rocking.

"Interesting skirt," he said appreciatively as he folded the newspaper away.

She stuck out one leg, lifting a portion of the skirt for better viewing. "I bought it from a lady here in town. She patched all these pieces together from scraps."

"I'd like to check out some of the crafts while I'm here. I caught just a glimpse of a few of them as we drove into town yesterday."

He had given her an excellent segue into the subject she wanted to discuss, she reflected, namely, the fact that he would be staying in town longer than he had originally intended. But he spoke up while she was still hesitating.

"You know, if you could capture the essence of an afternoon like this one for your hotel brochure, you'd book up years in advance and have multitudes clamoring at your front door."

Her gaze followed his to the vast green lawn, where red and orange leaves tumbled merrily. "No way. Afternoons such as this make me want to keep it all to myself, and Gran feels the same way."

He grinned. "I don't blame either of you one bit. In fact, I was just sitting here thinking how nice it would be if the football game went into overtime and the reunion group was delayed for a while."

She chuckled. "That *would* be nice."

He looked over at her. "Any chance?"

"Probably not. The other team is much better than theirs. More than likely, it'll be a one-sided game."

"Too bad."

His genuine appreciation of the quiet autumn afternoon came as a surprise to her, a very *nice* surprise. But she kept it to herself for fear he might accuse her of jumping to another conclusion about him. And he'd be right.

"What's wrong?"

She blinked. "What?"

"You're staring at me as if something's wrong."

Perhaps it had been a trick of the golden light, but for a split second Lion had looked completely at home there on her grandmother's porch in one of her rockers. He had looked as if he *belonged*. She quickly shook her head, giving him a negative reply, as well as trying to shake some sense into her head. "Nothing's wrong." No, she was positive it had been a trick of the light. "Listen, I wanted to tell you how glad I am that you decided to stay, though I'm sorry about the reason."

His brows shot up. "You're glad I'm staying? I thought I detected a touch of dismay from you this morning."

Her lips twisted ruefully. "You probably did, but it was short-lived. The truth is I'm glad we're going to get another chance."

He studied her with an assessing gaze. "I'm all for extra chances when it comes to you, but you're probably referring to something different than I am."

Determined not to let him shake her, she grinned. "You're probably right."

"Oh, there's no *probably* about it."

She kept her grin firmly in place. "Well, it's just that if you had left this morning, you would have left with a bad impression."

He cocked his head to one side. "How do you figure?"

She'd thought through what she wanted to say to him, but the glittering warmth in his eyes kept distracting her. She drew in a deep breath, then slowly let it out. "You would have left with a bad impression of me, of our whole encounter, because . . ."

"Because?"

"Because you were right about my jumping to conclusions about you. I did label you unfairly, and for that I'm very, very sorry."

"Well, hooray," he said, his voice soft and suddenly, disturbingly intimate. "Does that mean you're going to start—to use your words—to take me seriously?"

She took her time answering him, choosing her words with care. This morning, after he'd left the lobby with Bo, and after her grandmother had stated her preposterous notions, she'd searched her heart and mind about him. It had taken some doing and some time, but she'd finally been able, once again, to put him in a proper perspective and accept that he would be around, at least for another day. "You're a very nice, very interesting man, Lion, and I'm happy to have the additional time to get to know you better."

"I know there's an *and* or a *but* coming, so what is it?"

She shrugged. "*And*, as I said, I'm also happy to have the opportunity to tell you how sorry I am to have judged you simply on a first impression."

She was being as truthful as she knew how to be—she really was through judging him hastily. But there was also another truth she had no plans to divulge. She still viewed him as someone out of place, a Kevin Costner who had appeared unexpectedly in her backyard and who would soon be moving on. And there was no doubt in her mind that, while he was here, he would continue to come on to her—it was his nature. But her vow to remain unaffected by him hadn't changed. She could handle anything that he might do or say and have a great time in the process.

He slowly smiled. "You're a very unexpected woman, Gabi. Unexpected and intriguing."

Unexpected? Intriguing? Funny, she'd thought the same of him. But the two words were so far removed from how she viewed herself, she had to laugh. "Lion, I'm about as intriguing as an open book."

"Books are one of my passions."

She hadn't needed to hear his answer to know that he would be passionate about most things in his life, nor that he would be able to take an analogy of hers and turn it back on her. Moreover, in less time than it takes to blink, she'd known he could do or say something that would take her unawares, both mentally and physically. No judgment, just bone-deep intuition. Even now, when he was completely relaxed, a constant fire burned deep in his eyes. She cleared her throat. "I'd like to ask you something."

"Sure. What is it?"

Her grandmother believed he had extended his stay because of her. Though she didn't agree, she was curious enough to want to find out for sure. "I want to know the truth about your watch."

"The truth?"

The surprise that appeared on his face gave her a moment's pause. "Don't get me wrong. I understand how anyone would be concerned about being robbed. But it's hard for me to believe you'd stay over an extra day for a mere watch."

He shifted in the chair, angling his body toward her, and his expression darkened, intensified. But when he spoke, it was quietly, gently.

"First of all, Gabi, I didn't have a set schedule for the weekend, so the decision to stay wasn't that difficult to make. And next, and most important, the watch that's missing is not a *mere* watch. It was my father's and my grandfather's before him. Its value to me is incalculable."

"Oh . . . I'm sorry, I didn't know."

"There's no way you could have known."

True, she thought. Very true. But she was still having a tough time forgiving herself for even broaching the subject.

"My grandfather died twenty-one years ago and left the watch to my father, who always carried it," he said, unexpectedly continuing. "Then sixteen years ago both of my parents were killed in a private plane crash while flying to Switzerland. To this day I don't know why my father left the watch at home, but because he did, the watch passed to me. I don't wear it unless I'm in a three-piece suit, but I usually carry it with me in some way or another. This trip it was in my briefcase."

"I'm so sorry." Her words were barely audible.

He smiled gently. "It's all right."

"No, it's not. I had no right to question you, and I'm appalled at my bad manners."

He reached over and took her hand. "Your manners are fine, Gabi."

"No." She shook her head firmly. "However inadvertently, I still dredged up a subject that's very sad to you. It was inexcusable of me."

His hand tightened reassuringly on hers. "It was a very private, very personal tragedy, but it was also big news that was broadcast around the world. My cousins and I will probably never get over our family being wiped out like that, but we've all had to accept it and move on."

She looked at him. "Your cousins? You mean you had aunts and uncles who were killed too?"

"All of them. Violently and with one evil, vicious act—a bomb was planted on their plane. But I'm happy to be able to tell you that the person who was responsible has been brought to justice. It's been a long time, but we can all finally feel a measure of peace about the whole thing."

She blinked away the moisture she could feel welling in her eyes. "It's hard for me to even imagine the scope of such a tragedy."

He squeezed her hand. "I'm glad. It means you've been blessed with a happy life. Hey"—he reached a finger to her cheek and lifted away a tear that, despite her best efforts, had escaped—"it's too great a day for tears, Gabi."

"I know." She gave what she considered a discreet sniff. "And I really wasn't crying. Something must have gotten into my eyes."

"Oh, yeah?"

His grin told her that he wasn't fooled. "Yeah. And . . . I was also thinking about . . ."

"About?"

"How much pain you've been through."

An odd expression appeared on his face. Then all at once, he surged to his feet, pulling her with him. "Let's go for a walk."

"A walk?" She gestured toward the front door. "I should tell someone."

"Is Maggie around?"

"She's in the office with Bo."

"Does the phone ring in there?"

"Yes."

"Then let's go."

She had no idea why, but she couldn't stop the smile that spread across her face. "Sounds like a terrific idea."

FIVE

Lion realized he'd had a near-constant smile on his face for the past fifteen minutes. Gabi's doing, of course. Strolling beside him, delightfully unguarded and open, she'd laughed and chatted, and in the process, kept him entertained and, unknowingly, beguiled.

When they'd first started out, he'd adjusted his normally long stride to match her shorter one and the leisurely pace she'd chosen. If she had a destination in mind, he didn't know, nor did he much care. He was following her lead and, as she always seemed to, taking each moment as it came.

They'd made their way to the right side of the hotel and were heading toward the back lawn on a brick walkway, lined with yellow, orange, and rust-colored chrysanthemums. Not too far away, dark purple asters, crimson and mauve starflowers, and pale lilac crocuses filled other beds that curved and flowed around trees and birdbaths.

"So tell me about yourself," she said, as animated and bright as the day.

He barely stopped himself from doing a double take. "Weren't you just talking about a cocker spaniel you once had?"

"Uh-huh. His name was Rusty, not a very original name, since he was rust-colored, but then what can you expect? I was eight years old. Why?"

"No reason, really. I guess I wasn't ready for the abrupt change of subject." In fact, he'd been absorbed with simply looking at her, engrossed by the various expressions that had been chasing across her face, immersed in listening to the melody of her voice rather than the words she was saying.

Faint lines of puzzlement creased her brow. "I didn't think it was that abrupt."

"It probably wasn't." Acting on impulse enhanced by irresistible need, he reached out to smooth the tips of his fingers over the puzzle lines, then trail them down to the softness of her cheek. She made a faint sound, which sent warmth winding through him to pool in his lower abdomen. He dropped his hand. "At any rate, it's nothing to frown about."

"Do you have any pets?"

She might have rushed out the question, he reflected dryly, but she'd obviously recovered from his touch much quicker than he had. His fingertips still tingled with the feel of her skin. "Two golden retrievers."

"Golden retrievers are *beautiful* dogs. What are their names?"

He'd become so used to the sound of her laughter, and so curiously dependent on it, that he found himself saying something he hoped would make her laugh. "Davie and Dougie."

She burst out laughing. "You're kidding."

Her laughter was warm and luminous, almost liquid with glitter and sparkle. If it were a river, he'd want to swim out to the middle of it and then float on its current. "Hey, I didn't name them. My sister did."

Her mouth fell open in clear astonishment. "You have a sister?"

Now it was his turn to laugh, something he realized he did a great deal around her. "What did you think? That my parents were so traumatized by me, they decided no more kids? Or maybe that I had automatically drowned any sibling at birth?"

An easy smile spread across her face. "Nothing that drastic. Actually I hadn't thought about it one way or the other until you mentioned it. But you're a very self-contained, very complete person, Lion, which makes you seem separate unto yourself, as if you have no strings that connect you to anything or anyone." She paused, then hurried to add, "And that is not intended to be a label of any kind, or a judgment. I said you *seem* separate, I didn't say you *were*."

Without breaking stride, he bowed in her direction. "I'm quite impressed with this new open-mindedness of yours."

Mischief lit her eyes. "Oh, good. Then all my effort hasn't been wasted."

Impressed was only the beginning of a whole range of emotions she made him feel. "But you're wrong."

"Well, I don't want to disagree with you, but I *do* disagree with you."

"What a shock." It was incredibly effortless to joke with her, *almost* as effortless as it was to want her.

She abruptly halted beside a rosebush, heavy with peach-colored blooms. "Look at these gorgeous roses. This bush has done so well this year. It's been blooming since spring, but these are probably the last of the year." She picked one, held it to her nose, then lifted it to his. "Nice, huh?"

"Nice." A swift surge of desire kicked him in the gut. Her skin had felt like a rose petal, and the mere memory made him yearn to touch her again, to slide his hands beneath her clothes to the fullness of her breasts, where, no doubt, her skin would be even softer.

She started walking again while he stood rooted to the spot, battling the suddenly urgent need to grab her, lay her down on the grass, and make love to her right then and there. He was in danger of coming apart at the seams, he realized, while she was serene, composed, and entirely unaware of what he was going through. For his own peace of mind, he chose to laugh instead of swear.

She threw an inquiring glance back at him, and he hurried to catch up to her.

She nodded toward the far edge of the hotel

where two men sat on the grass, a tall red thermal jug beside each of them, along with a large toolbox. "Bill and Mike. They're doing a bit of repairing for us, putting in new windows and patching a couple of holes."

"I heard their hammering earlier," he said, relieved that his voice sounded even and unshaken.

"Yeah. Unfortunately a certain amount of maintenance has to go on all the time with a hotel of this age."

"That's understandable." Trying to distract himself from the hard need for her that continued to hold him in its grip, he pointed to the white Victorian-style gazebo he had first seen from the window of his suite. "The gazebo is really something."

"Isn't it? Everyone loves it, and there's another one in a clearing in the woods that's really nice, too, but not too many people venture that far."

A path branched to their right and meandered through a sprawling flower and vegetable garden. At the path's end, an arched arbor trellis gracefully bore the weight of scarlet morning glories.

Twirling the peach-colored rose between her fingers, Gabi stayed on the main path. "So tell me about your sister. What's her name?"

"Yasmine."

"What a beautiful name."

"She's a beautiful girl."

She looked up at him, her lovely brown eyes snapping with intelligence and curiosity. "There was a wonderful softness in your voice just then. I can tell you love her very much."

"Yes, I do."

"Then you're close?"

He nodded. "And I'm also very close to my entire family. So see? There goes your self-contained, no-strings theory."

"Not really." With a graceful sweep of her hand, she combed her hair back from her face. "But I probably chose the wrong phrase to describe the feeling I get from you. The truth is, I've never known anyone like you. You have such a strong presence, you practically carry your own force field with you. And by the way, that's not a judgment, that's a fact."

He knew exactly what and who he was, and he was very comfortable in his own skin. So it wasn't *what* she said that surprised him, but the fact that she had said it at all. "You make me sound . . ."

"Formidable? Well, you *are*, and you can*not* make me believe that you don't know it."

He'd been called that, plus much more and much worse, but it was *her* interpretation of him that interested him, interested him to a highly unusual degree. With a hand on her arm he drew her to a halt beside him. "So you think I'm formidable?"

"Most definitely."

He dropped his gaze to her lips, bare of lipstick, the sight so tantalizing he could barely stand it. He returned his gaze to her eyes. "Tell me you're intimidated by me—tell me and make me believe it."

"Of course I'm not."

"Then you can't really believe that I'm formidable."

She chuckled. "Sure I can. And by the way, who's making judgments now?"

Sunlight lay gently on her skin, touching it with a natural gilt, and caught in her hair, highlighting it with streaks of gold. Every time he looked at her, he saw something new. Slowly he shook his head, his expression wry. "And all this time I've been consciously going easy on you."

"Why would you do that?"

"Excellent question." He took her hand and sensed rather than felt her stiffen. But she didn't pull away. With a gentle tug on her hand, he resumed their stroll. "What do you think the answer is?"

"I wouldn't even hazard a guess."

"And here I thought you had all the answers."

Her laughter pealed out across the afternoon. "That was yesterday. Today, I'm *much* smarter."

"Smarter and more lovely every time I look at you." He noted the faint color that crept up her neck.

"Thank you." She glanced away.

"What's this?" He reached over and lightly skimmed his fingers up her throat, following the path of the color. "I would never have pegged you for the type to blush at a simple compliment."

"I'm not." She pulled her hand from his.

"Glad to hear it." He grinned. "I didn't embarrass you, did I?"

"No."

"Or make you nervous?"

"No."

"And I can't be the first man to give you a compliment."

"No." In an almost absentminded gesture, she pressed her fingers to her throat where he had touched, then abruptly dropped her hand. "So tell me about your sister. Is she younger?"

"Yes." He went along with the change of subject, mainly because if she'd decided to ask him why he kept touching her, he wouldn't have been able to explain. He only knew the urge to have her was growing stronger and more impossible to resist by the minute.

"I always thought it was wonderful, having a big brother."

"I'll bet you bossed yours around like crazy."

"No, I did not," she said, amused.

His brows shot up. "Oh, yeah? You couldn't prove it by me."

"Does Yasmine boss you around?"

"If she does, I have to say I haven't noticed."

"That means she's either very smart or very nice."

"She's both, actually." A movement near the edge of the woods caught his attention and he discovered a pair of dark eyes staring back at him. A moment later he saw a dark-eyed mask and a bushy-ringed tail. "There's a raccoon watching us."

"So there is. That's Rocky."

He chuckled as he got the Beatles reference. "Rocky Raccoon."

"Right. Oops, there he goes, back into the woods."

"I think I saw him early this morning—him or one of his relatives."

"It was probably him. He's the most sociable raccoon we've ever had around here, which makes him a real favorite, not to mention pest. In his honor, we now keep a lock on our trash. But we consider ourselves very lucky to have wildlife so close. Sometimes in the mornings, deer come out to graze on the lawn. I love to watch them."

"Are the animals used to people?"

"Some, not all. We strongly recommend that our guests leave them alone." She smiled. "We tell them it's for their safety, but quite honestly, we're more concerned about the safety of the animals. We love having them around, and the last thing we want is for them to be bothered."

"Makes perfect sense."

"Well, I do try." She pointed to a path that led into the woods. "Let's go this way."

"You lead and I will follow."

She threw a suspicious glance his way. "Are you making fun of me again?"

"Never." Solemnly he laid his hand over his heart. "I promise."

"Uh-huh." Her tone was dry. "Right."

A squirrel suddenly darted into their path. Seeing them, he went motionless, his mouth bulging with acorns.

"Hello, little one," Gabi said in a soft croon, then laughed as he dashed away into the woods. "He can't stop to talk, he's got things to do."

"And acorns to store up for the winter. Smart squirrel, planning ahead."

"Well, thank goodness. His family is depending on him."

"He's got a family?"

"Sure. Two girls and a boy, not to mention the missus."

Being teased by Gabi was like being bathed in warm honey, he reflected. It was a sweet, intimate, and surprisingly sensual experience. "Speaking of family—"

"Yours, mine, or the squirrel's?"

He grinned. "Yours. Tell me about Maggie and the good sheriff."

"What do you want to know?"

"Well, to start with, Maggie made it very clear this morning that she doesn't want him to do much investigating at all. In fact, she threw a lot of roadblocks in his way. Why?"

"She just can't stand to think that anyone would steal from the hotel. She considers the hotel her home and her employees and guests her personal friends."

"Admirable, but not the best way to go in this situation."

"Don't worry about it. Bo's very, very good, both at getting around her and doing his job. He'll get your watch back if anyone can."

"I'm counting on it."

"I know you are."

The compassion in her tone drew his gaze. Nice, he thought, but it wasn't her sympathy he wanted.

"What's the history between Bo and Maggie? Obviously there is some."

Her smile flashed back to life. "A *long* history. He was her older brother's best friend, and she had a terrific crush on him all the time she was growing up. Of course, she'd never admit that to him, not then and certainly not now."

He nodded. "Tactical error, I'm guessing?"

"You got it. Anyway, I think Bo saw her as just the kid sister of his best friend—you know, someone to tease when he was in the mood, but otherwise ignore. In time, he went off to college, joined the marines, fell in love, and eventually married. Gran grew up and, in the process, grew out of the crush, and in time met my granddad and tumbled head over heels in love for real."

"Your granddad is the one who built the hotel?"

"His father did, actually. My great-grandfather. But about the time Granddad and Gran married, he took over the running of the hotel. He knew she wanted to stay in the town where she had grown up, and the hotel provided them with both an income and a lovely home. They were madly in love until the day he died."

"So when did Bo come back into the picture?"

"He never really left the picture. After he got out of the marines, he came back here and raised his family. He and his wife were good friends of Gran and Granddad. But he lost his wife about eight years ago and not too long after that Granddad died."

"That's been a while."

"Getting over the death of a spouse is not an easy thing. It takes time."

"But Bo is pursuing her now, right?"

"Oh, yeah, definitely. But as you probably gathered, she's resisting."

"Why?"

She laughed. "General principle, I think."

He nodded with understanding. "She's getting him back for all those years when she was growing up and he didn't look twice at her."

"That's about the size of it. Hell hath no fury "

"Like a Maggie scorned, huh?"

"To put it mildly. But they're both having a great time. Actually we all are. The maneuvering between the two of them has been highly entertaining."

"I'll bet." The sound of flowing water reached his ears, then a few moments later he saw the source, a creek with a wooden bridge arcing over it. He followed Gabi to the middle of the bridge, leaned against the railing, and gazed down at the clear water as it flowed over stones and rocks.

Listening, he heard the breeze rustling through the leaves and the occasional song of an unseen bird. Here, the air was cooler, more fragrant, nature more immediate. He'd seen many beautiful places; he even owned property that possessed awe-inspiring scenery. But the beauty here was different. Rather than taking your breath away, it soothed with its serenity and grace.

He turned to face Gabi and was stunned anew by how much he wanted her. *Still.* Instead of lessening or even disappearing, his need for her had grown until now he could think of very little else. Very soon he was going to have to do something about it. "This place has a secret feeling about it," he said quietly. "We could be miles from the nearest person instead of yards."

She nodded. "That's one of the reasons I've always loved it. When I was young, I used to run away and come here."

"Run away? As in run away from home?"

"Sure." She grinned. "Whenever I'd get mad, I'd stage a great dramatic scene, throw a few of my favorite toys in a bag, and head straight for here."

"And what would your parents do?"

"Nothing. They always knew exactly where I was and that I'd be back before sundown." With her hands grasping the railing, she leaned backward. "I spent many a happy hour down there on the banks of the creek, dangling my feet in the water and building castles and forts with the rocks."

"Castles and forts? A budding architect, huh?"

She laughed. "When you're young, it's hard to be consistent."

"It's hard when you're an adult too."

Still grasping the railing, she swayed back and forth and studied Lion from beneath her lashes. She'd always felt at peace here, but today she felt nervous and exhilarated. Throughout the afternoon Lion had been gentle and seemingly at ease. But his presence alone created a disturbance in the air around her.

More than once, his brute force had reached out and caressed her, though he had done nothing at all.

It was time to face the strong possibility that she just might be in trouble.

Suddenly he wrapped a hand around her upper arm and turned her to him. "What's wrong?" she asked, startled.

"Nothing. Everything."

His expression was sharper, grimmer, and more frustrated than it had been since she'd met him, she noted warily. "I don't understand."

"Don't feel bad, because neither do I."

He framed her face with strong, lean fingers. Gazing up into his eyes, she saw the glittering shards of a fiery ruthlessness. On her skin, she felt the blistering burn of his touch. She should break away from him, she thought, and run faster than she'd ever run before. But she waited, curious, mesmerized.

"This afternoon has been wonderful, Gabi," he said in a heated, grit-textured voice. "I can't remember when I've had a better time."

"I've enjoyed it too."

"I'm glad. But the thing is—it hasn't been nearly enough for me. I want more."

"More?"

"More time with you," he murmured, beginning to slowly lower his head toward her. "And much more of you."

His warm breath fluttered over her lips, then his mouth covered hers in a complete possession. She stiffened, unprepared, even though somehow, some-way, she had known that this kiss would come.

His lips were firm, sure, but he didn't rush her. Instead the kiss was almost leisurely, the pace allowing her to become accustomed to his nearness, his taste. Smart of him, she thought as she felt herself slowly begin to relax. Dumb of her.

His thumbs smoothed over her cheeks, hypnotizing her, then his hands dropped to her shoulders and pulled her closer against him. She drew in a deep breath, and his clean, musky scent shot to her brain, swiftly followed by a blast of heat. New tension sprang up inside her, new nerves began to clang, but the strong beat of his heart against her chest reassured her. She slid her arms around his neck, threaded her fingers into his hair, and gave herself up to the enveloping strength of his body and the forceful power of his will.

A rich, full-blown desire burst open in her, textured by a coil of unfamiliar emotions. She felt as if she'd been hit by a lightning bolt out of a blue sky, and she didn't have a clue how to begin to cope.

Hearing a moan, she realized it had come from her. It was a sound of pleasure and of distress, both feelings equally strong. Her desire for him collided with a need for safety. A longing to kiss him for hours and then make love to him smashed into an instinct to run. She pressed her hands against his chest, savoring the strength and the heat, but at the same time pushing him away.

Slowly, gradually, he broke the exquisite seal of

their joined lips and drew his head back. Looking up into his eyes, she saw a blazing, unsettling mixture of fire and steel.

"I was right," he said harshly. "I definitely want more."

She could think of nothing to say. She felt dazed, knocked off her feet, in fact, almost *assaulted.* He'd only kissed her, but it was as if he'd consumed her.

She'd known from the first he was a predator. She'd also known she would be his prey. Yet she hadn't resisted him. How extremely foolish of her.

She lifted a shaking hand and was momentarily confused as to whether she was reaching out to him or trying to ward him off. She dropped her arm to her side. "I've got to get back."

"Running, Gabi?"

"No, I'm walking." She drew in a deep, ragged breath. "Very fast and starting right now. Good-bye." She managed to take only three steps before he spoke again, stopping her in her tracks.

"It's not good-bye, Gabi. I'm staying—remember?"

She glanced over her shoulder at him. "Of course. See you soon."

"Count on it," he said. "Count on it."

Lion watched her until she disappeared from his view into the woods, then he leaned back against the railing. But he didn't relax. He couldn't. His body still pulsed for her and his mind raced.

Now he knew. Now he understood.

The only surprise was that it had taken him so long to discover the truth.

He was in love with Gabi.

He'd been shaken by the wreck and then immediately been knocked breathless by Gabi. Under the circumstances, he supposed he could be excused for being a bit slow on the uptake.

He wasn't the type of man who automatically lusted after any reasonably attractive woman. Being born a Damaron meant he had had to learn early to think with his head, not his hormones. Not an easy lesson, especially during his teenage years, but nevertheless he had mastered it. Because along with the wealth and power had come heavy responsibility. As a result, the relationships he'd had with women had followed certain rules that involved mutual safety, pleasure, respect, and the understanding that there would be no commitment.

And then Gabi had come along.

He'd wanted her immediately. What red-blooded man wouldn't? But she'd also bemused, confounded, and irritated him. And *always* she'd fascinated him. Her effect on him was out of the ordinary, and she'd set churning inside him so many different emotions and feelings, he hadn't been able to see that he was falling in love with her.

But as soon as his lips had touched hers, he had known. Fire had flared in his belly, and she'd melted against him like sweet, hot honey, and the very certain knowledge that he loved her had come crashing down on him.

Somehow, someway, when he'd been busy trying to figure her out, Gabi had stolen his heart. And now he had a problem.

She didn't love him.

Oh, she was curious about him, and she enjoyed being with him. She liked to tease him and laugh at and with him. She'd even responded to his kisses.

But she didn't love him.

That would change, though. It had to. Simply having her, making love to her, wasn't going to come close to satisfying him now. He wouldn't be *completely* satisfied until she loved him and she had given him her heart.

SIX

As Gabi neared the back of the hotel she heard voices and realized with a shock that the reunion group had returned. She'd had no idea it was that late, and hastened her steps along the brick pathway. She would be needed, and she was anxious to learn if Bo had made any progress with his investigation.

She also was hoping that a hotel full of guests would distract her from Lion.

But as she passed the peach rosebush where she and Lion had stopped on their walk, her steps faltered. She had to concede there wasn't a distraction in the world strong enough to take her mind off Lion. Her reaction to him had left her thoroughly shaken. She could still taste him on her lips and feel the effects of his kisses throughout her body.

Running from him wasn't the answer. Neither was attempting to distract herself. No, she was going to have to face what had happened and deal with it.

And she would. *Later*.

Rounding the corner of the hotel, she encountered a touch-football game in progress on the front law. A few moments of watching was all she needed to know the game was long on high jinks and short on rules. Not too far away, she saw Camilla sitting on the grass with her skirt spread around her, tarot cards before her, and three of her female classmates listening intently to what she was saying. Others of the reunion group were gathered on the porch, enjoying late-afternoon drinks and conversation.

"Did your team win?" she called out as she climbed the front steps. Thumbs turned down and cheerfully negative replies flew. She waved. "Sorry."

Inside the lobby, more of their group milled around. And over by the reception desk, her grandmother was laughing with Lawrence Duncan.

But her personal radar was obviously working full blast, because as Gabi approached, Maggie swiveled toward her. "Ah, there you are, darling. I've been wondering where you were."

"Sorry I was gone so long."

Maggie's gaze sharpened. "Is that a flush on your face?"

"I was hurrying. Hello, Mr. Duncan. How are you this afternoon?"

"I couldn't be better, Gabi. I was just telling your grandmother how much I'm enjoying my stay here. Fall in Arkansas is something one has to experience to really appreciate."

"That's very true and I'm glad you're having a

good time. Gran, is there something specific I need to do or check on?" She'd have to wait until the two of them were alone to ask about Bo's investigation.

"No, but I do need a minute of your time." Maggie turned to bestow a particularly lovely smile on the Englishman. "Lawrence, would you please excuse me? I need to have a word with my granddaughter."

"Certainly. No problem." He flicked back his immaculate white cuff for a glance at his watch. "Shall I meet you down here at seven, then?"

"Perfect. I'll be looking forward to it."

"Looking forward to what?" Gabi asked curiously, as soon as he had moved off.

"Lawrence and I are having dinner together this evening."

"Dinner? *Why?*" As gregarious and friendly as her grandmother was, Gabi had never known her to dine with a guest.

"Because, darling, he *asked* me"—Maggie spoke with exaggerated slowness as if it would help Gabi better understand—"and because he's a very nice man, not to mention distinguished and good-looking. Now tell me what happened on your walk with Lion."

"Nothing happened. Where's Bo?"

"Gone, I'm glad to say. Where's Lion?"

"Bo's gone? I thought he'd be staying longer."

"I thought Lion would be staying longer too. You didn't run him off, did you?"

"Of course not. Did Bo find out anything?"

"Of course not." Abruptly, Maggie grabbed her arm, tugged her around the reception desk, and pushed her into the office. "We seem to be carrying on two conversations at once. I vote we eliminate yours and concentrate on mine." She shut the door behind them. "Okay, now what happened with Lion?"

"I already told you, Gran. *Nothing* happened."

"Well, how *extremely* vexing." With a heavy sigh, Maggie leaned against the edge of the desk, crossed her arms at her waist, and fixed Gabi with a level gaze. "And I'm trying to decide who I'm more disappointed in—you or Lion."

"Give me a break, Gran." Lion was the last thing she wanted to talk about, she reflected tiredly.

No, give *me* a break." With a dramatic flourish, Maggie threw up her hands. "Since when is it a crime to be concerned about your granddaughter? Since *never*, that's when."

Gabi rolled her eyes. "Why did you even bother to bring me in here? You answer your own questions."

"Uh-huh, well, I can also tell you something else." She wagged a finger at her. "It's a *huge* responsibility to be your grandmother, along with being extremely frustrating. I want so much for you, yet what do you do? *Nothing*. That's what. You refuse to cooperate."

"The very *moment* I find the one great love of my life, I *promise* I will start to cooperate. Okay? Now tell me what Bo found out."

Maggie slowly shook her head, clearly disheartened. "You're still practically a virgin. And frankly, my darling, I'm at a loss to know what I should do about you."

Gabi's mind went blank. "Bo found out I'm practically a virgin?"

Maggie frowned. "Bo couldn't find the hand at the end of his arm. Try to pay attention, Gabriela. You're practically a virgin, and—"

"I'm *not* a virgin."

"Technically, maybe not."

"Technically?" She and her grandmother had had many odd conversations over the years, but this one topped them all.

Maggie gave a dismissive wave of her hand. "Oh, I know there was that young man, Morris or Martin or—"

"Mark. His name was *Mark*, as you well know. I brought him here many times. And he was very nice."

"I never liked him."

"*I* did."

"He wasn't the *one*, and I told you so at the time."

"Yes, you did. Often."

"And you might have had sex with him once or twice—"

"For most of that summer."

"But your heart wasn't involved. Matt—"

"Mark."

"Wasn't your one great love. Lion *is*."

Gabi felt like hitting the back of her head against the door. It was either that or scream. "No, Gran, he isn't."

"He *is*. I have a *real* feeling about him. And if

you'd just quit being so stubborn and open yourself up to the possibilities—"

"Would you *please* just drop this subject?"

Maggie's expression turned puzzled. "Why would I want to do something that would be so detrimental to you?"

She was getting a headache, Gabi realized. "We've talked about this before, Gran. If Lion doesn't leave tomorrow, he'll leave the next day, and then I'll never see him again."

"Well, for goodness' sakes, Gabriela, how long do you need anyway?" She held up her hand. "No, don't answer. Knowing you, you might say a year, and the truth is, if you do it right, whatever time you have will be long enough. As a matter of fact, I remember spending one really, amazing weekend with your grandfather, which was when—"

"Please, no sordid details. I'd like to maintain a few illusions about my grandparents."

Maggie's eyes narrowed on her. "Those sordid details happen to be very precious to me, Gabriela. Though now that I think about it, that particular story might not have been the best example anyway. At any rate, getting back to the point I was trying to make, I'm not asking you to commit to a lifelong relationship this weekend—unless, of course, you really want to."

"Careful, Gran. You're about to let me make a decision."

"As long as you make the right one." Maggie pushed away from the desk, went over to her, and grasped her arms. "*All* I'm asking is that you give yourself the *opportunity* to experience what could well turn out to be, at the very least, a great passion." She lightly shook her. "For goodness' sake, child, life doesn't give many second chances. Take this one while you can."

Gabi had to grin. "No matter how romantic you make it sound, you're still talking about a one-night stand."

"Not necessarily." Maggie dropped her hands and shrugged. "It could be two or three nights. The point is—"

"Never mind. I'm not up to another one of your points." Gabi sidestepped her grandmother and began to move around the room, hoping the activity would ease her headache and help her think more clearly. "You do know, don't you, that your advice would horrify every other grandmother in the world?"

"What is there? Some Grannie Union I don't know about?" Her brow creased with concern, Maggie followed Gabi with her gaze. "Sweetheart, I know I'm probably saying this very badly, but I'm just so afraid you're going to end up with serious regrets. Lion is an extraordinary man, and I don't understand why you took one look at him and decided he wasn't for you."

"Then we're even, because I don't understand why you took one look at him and decided I should go after him."

"You wouldn't have to go very far, Gabriela. I've seen the way he looks at you."

Gabi made an abrupt turn and stopped directly in front of her grandmother. "Okay, here's the deal. It's obvious you and I are never going to agree about Lion, so we need to drop the subject and move on. And *you*—you need to quit worrying about me, and while you're at it, you need to trust my instincts on this." She put her arms around her and gave her a hug. "I love you, Gran, and I do listen to you, but in this case"—she straightened away—"I *know* what I'm doing."

"I hope you do," Maggie said, her expression as worried as ever. "I really hope you do."

"I do." She'd whispered the words to herself, she realized. "I do," she said aloud.

The first person Gabi saw when she left the office was Lion, making his way across the crowded lobby. Her heart flip-flopped. With his exotic coloring and potent masculinity, Lion made all the other men in the area look faded and anemic.

A strong wave of doubt hit her. Did she *really* know what she was doing?

Suddenly, without once having looked at her, Lion changed directions and headed straight for her. It was almost as if he had *heard* her thoughts, she reflected, unnerved.

"What's wrong?" he asked as soon as he reached her.

"Why would you think anything is wrong?"

He touched her cheek, his fingers lingering on her skin. "You're pale."

"I'm fine."

"She's not fine," Maggie said, coming out of the office behind her, all signs of concern gone. "As a matter of fact, Gabi's quite obstinate. Getting her to accept my advice is a feat equivalent to convincing the Sphinx that the other side of the pyramid would be a better location."

Lion's gaze held steady on Gabi. "You have a problem you need advice on?"

"No, but that doesn't stop her."

"What can I do, Lion?" Maggie asked, a quiver in her voice. "I'm just an old woman. No one listens to me anymore."

He grinned. "Maggie, you're outrageous."

"At *last*, a man who appreciates me."

As tempted as she was to laugh, Gabi refrained because she knew it wouldn't help her headache. "If you two will excuse me, I have some things I have to do."

Lion put a staying hand on her arm. "Have dinner with me tonight?"

Fortunately she'd already considered her evening schedule and didn't have to think too hard for an answer. "I'm sorry, but I have to work tonight."

"No, you don't," Maggie said, cheerfully throwing a wrench into her plans. "Everything is covered."

"Aren't you having dinner with Mr. Duncan?" she asked, perplexed.

"Yes, but it doesn't matter. I've made arrangements so that you and I can both have the night off."

"But we have the reunion dinner dance scheduled tonight. If you're not working, I should be."

"Nonsense. How will the staff ever learn responsibility if you and I are always hovering over them?"

Gabi's mouth dropped open. Her grandmother just kept topping herself.

"Then it's settled," Lion said with a satisfied smile. "I'll see you in a couple of hours, Gabi. We can meet in the Pump Room."

"Sure. Fine. Whatever." She'd figure it all out later, she promised herself. For now she badly needed to get away from both her grandmother and Lion and be alone. "Excuse me."

His fingers tightened around her arm, and his gaze searched her face. "You really don't look well. Are you sure you're all right?"

Maggie snapped to attention. "You aren't coming down with something, are you, darling?"

"No, no—I've just got a slight headache."

"Then go lie down and rest," Maggie said. "And if you need anything, call me."

"I will." If only Lion would release her arm. She looked up at him inquiringly.

"Take care of yourself," he murmured, finally letting her go.

She nodded. Then without another word, she left.

Gabi sank into the steaming, lavender-scented bathwater, rested her head on the tub's rim, and sighed with pleasure. The rest of the hotel might be bursting with activity, but all was quiet here in her rooms. Little by little, she could feel herself relaxing, and already her headache was better.

Now if she could just get her mind to turn off . . .

But again and again her thoughts returned to Lion.

Her grandmother was truly convinced that he was the one great love of her life. But she didn't believe it. She *couldn't*.

Where Lion was concerned, she agreed with her grandmother on only one thing: He was an extraordinary man.

It would be a long, long time before she'd be able to forget the afternoon she'd spent with him. The feel of his touches had submerged into her and somehow become a part of her. Even the warm soapy water in which she was soaking wasn't enough to wash away the feelings, the sensations.

She heard a faint noise in the other room, and thinking that her grandmother had probably come to check on her, she sat up. "Gran?" There was no answer. After a couple of moments she decided she'd been mistaken about the noise and slid back down into the water. Once more her thoughts returned to Lion.

Accepting his dinner invitation hadn't been a smart decision, but it had been an inevitable one.

Truthfully, she would have found it extremely difficult to do anything else tonight but be with him.

Lion had turned out to be a compulsion, easier to give in to than resist. Even in the quiet of her rooms, six floors away from him, she could feel his energy and force like a pressure system against her skin.

He had come into her calm, happy life, disrupting and disturbing, heating her blood and the very air around her, making it practically impossible for her to think of anything or anyone but him. Hard as she tried, she couldn't ignore him and she couldn't keep him in perspective.

She could see no high ground anywhere.

So while he was here, her only recourse was to try to control what she could and not worry about what she couldn't. And most important, she needed to flow and bend with whatever happened between them. Otherwise she'd break.

"I'm sorry." Gabi automatically gave the apology as she turned to the person she'd bumped into. "Oh, Camilla, I'm sorry. I didn't see you."

"It's hard to watch where you're going in here." Camilla gestured around to her former schoolmates, who were thronging the lobby in their dinner-dance finery.

With a sweep of her hand, Gabi indicated the spangly combs and daringly diaphanous dress Camilla was wearing. "Even in a crowd you're a standout to-night. You look lovely."

"Thank you, and so do you. But"—Camilla's gaze grew thoughtful—"you're not having a good time, are you?"

"Oh, sure I am."

"No," she said firmly. "Your aura is still very, very disturbed."

"I see. Well, I appreciate your concern—"

"Hold on—I have *terrific* news for you, but I didn't know it until you bumped into me."

"You mean, just a moment ago?" Gabi asked, wondering if she looked as confused as she felt.

Camilla nodded enthusiastically. "It was the *contact* with you that enabled me to *feel* that you already have the answer within you to resolve your disturbance." She spread out her hands and her smile was searchlight bright. "Now all you have to do is figure out what it is you know. Great news, huh?"

Gabi went for the path of least resistance. "I'll say, and thank you once again."

"Anytime," Camilla said as a friend drew her into a nearby group.

Camilla was an interesting, likable woman, Gabi reflected, then promptly forgot her as she entered the Pump Room and discovered that it was even more packed than the lobby. She craned her neck, trying to find Lion, but she couldn't see him. Then she felt an electric intensity touch her skin.

She couldn't *see* Lion, but she could *feel* him, she reflected with amazement.

As if the feeling were a ribbon stretched between

them, she followed it to where he sat at the bar. "Hello."

"Hello, yourself." His long arm wrapped around her waist and drew her in between his hard thighs. "You look beautiful," he said huskily, and pressed his mouth to her ear and then to her forehead.

"Thank you." His greeting left her fighting to catch her breath, but she was immeasurably pleased by the compliment. After a great deal of consideration, she'd chosen to wear a little green silk dress with thin straps that angled across her shoulders and crisscrossed her back. But battling last-minute nerves, she'd elected to cover the bareness with a matching cashmere cardigan.

Lion ran a casually caressing, unnervingly possessive hand down her back as if he were savoring the sensual feel of the cashmere, and her body beneath it. Then keeping his hand at her waist, he offered her a glass with the other. "Drink?"

She glanced at it. "You ordered the springwater?"

"I thought I should at least try it, since it's what made this area famous."

"And?"

He set the water aside and lifted another glass, this one filled with whiskey. "Fortunately I had the foresight to order something else at the same time."

"That was not only farsighted of you, but very wise. It tastes awful, doesn't it?"

"Horrible."

She smiled. "My grandfather had a glass every single day of his life, but between you and me, I think it was more show for his guests than it was any love of the water."

His gaze lowered to her lips, lingered for several moments, then slowly returned to her eyes. "I've had a hell of a time the past few hours, keeping myself away from your room." He pulled her closer and clasped his hands together behind her back. "Not only was I very worried about you, I missed you like crazy."

For balance, for defense, she braced her hands against his chest and then was seduced by the warm strength beneath her palms. In a room filled with people, she was aware only of him. "My headache's gone."

"It was more than just a *slight* headache, wasn't it?"

"I never get headaches. I'm not sure why . . ." Her voice trailed off and she shrugged self-consciously. "I think I just needed a little rest."

"That was apparent, and by the way, the only thing that kept me away."

A love song played on the jukebox, gentle and melodic, and the intimate lighting fostered the illusion that they were alone in their own private world—unquestionably, a risky place for her to be. "You can take your drink into the dining room if you'd like."

"I'm pretty comfortable here."

She was, too, dangerously so. Her body felt treacherously pliant, boneless. She could feel reality slipping away from her.

Chris, one of the newer bartenders, appeared across the bar from her. "Evening, Gabi. Didn't mean to ignore you. Can I get you something?"

Silently she blessed him for breaking the spell into which she'd been so willingly tumbling. "No, thanks. We're about to go eat."

"Let me know if you change your mind." With a nod, Chris ambled off.

Gabi looked around her. The crowd had thinned out, which meant the dinner dance was right on schedule. She and Lion should leave, too, before they really were alone. She eased herself out of his embrace.

He grinned. "I gather you're ready to eat?"

"Yes."

Lion scrawled his name across the check, then stood. "I had a rental car sent over earlier. Would you like to get out, maybe try another restaurant?"

She shook her head. "I need to stay here."

"Are you sure?" He eyed her curiously. "I thought you might like a change of scenery."

"There's too much going on here tonight for me to feel easy about leaving, no matter what Gran says."

An intriguing, blood-warming smile slowly spread across his face. "I'm flattered you feel the need to have the security of a hotel full of people between us."

"I don't," she said, surprised at his take on her decision. "I *need* to stay."

"It's all right, Gabi. I'm good at challenges."

She almost groaned aloud. If the need for security

had played a part in her decision to stay in for dinner, it had been unconscious on her part. But either way, the last thing she wanted was for Lion to view her as a challenge. Presented with a challenge, he would be unstoppable.

SEVEN

Pausing in the doorway of the restaurant, Gabi gazed at the sole patrons, a young couple she recognized as local. "It's even quieter in here than it was last night."

"The service should be spectacular," Lion said at her side.

"I can't guarantee it. For all I know, Gran pulled all the waiters from here and shifted them to the dinner dance."

"That would be okay too."

She glanced up at him. "Bad service would be okay?"

"As long as I'm with you."

It was getting harder and harder for her to shrug away his come-ons. Thankfully, he didn't seem to notice she was stuck for a reply.

"Speaking of Maggie," he began. "She and her date don't appear to be here yet."

"She may have decided to eat out."

Beverly strolled up. "Good evening," the hostess said with a welcoming smile. "Are you two coming in?"

Lion casually slipped a hand into the pocket of his slacks and turned a teasing smile on her. "Do you think you can find us a table?"

Beverly blushed, but to her credit, she managed a chuckle. "That's why they pay me the big bucks."

With the brunt of Lion's attention temporarily off her, Gabi felt free to consider more practical matters. "Did Gran leave a waiter in here?"

Beverly nodded. "Ray. He's in the kitchen, helping with the Koslows' order." She gestured toward the young couple who were holding hands across the table. "They're celebrating their second wedding anniversary tonight."

"Please give them our best wishes," Lion said. "And send a bottle of champagne to them with our regards and add it to my tab."

Twice, he'd said *our*, Gabi reflected, as if the two of them were a couple. Twice, her pulses had jumped. She'd be a nervous wreck by the end of the evening if she couldn't stop reacting to everything he did or said. "Has it been this quiet in here all evening?"

Beverly nodded. "Pretty much. Not even the Wentworths showed up, and they've eaten in here every night since they arrived. They must have decided to try another place."

"Has Gran been in?"

"Not yet." With a wave of her hand, Beverly indicated the nearly empty restaurant. "You two pick yourself out a table, and I'll let Ray know he's got some new customers."

Lion placed a warm hand at Gabi's back and guided her to the table they'd had the night before. "Is this all right?" he asked, pulling out a chair for her.

"It's fine." She sat down, then watched him move around the table and settle into the opposite chair. She mentally braced herself for what she knew would happen next.

Sure enough, as was his way, Lion focused the full power of his attention on her. "Are you going to order for us again tonight?"

"It depends." She reached for the menu, though she knew it by heart. "What are you in the mood for?"

"You. Alone. In bed with me."

She'd known Lion would pick up where he'd left off this afternoon, yet even so, she'd been blindsided by his words. "How about the prime rib?"

He nodded solemnly. "That sounds good—for now."

For now. As she motioned to Ray the remark continued to ring in her ears. Purposely, she took as long as possible to give their order, allowing herself time to restore her composure. It worked, and when Ray finally walked off, she attempted to steer the conversation to a safer course. "Have you talked with Bo about his investigation into the theft of your watch?"

"Yes. Bo called me right before I came downstairs.

He wanted to touch base with me, since he'd had to leave before you and I returned from our walk."

The reminder of their walk—and their shared kisses—struck unwanted dents into her newly gained composure. It was also a reminder that Lion would go along with her change of subject only as long as *he* wanted to. "What did he say?"

"That he's coming back tonight."

"Tonight? I wonder if Gran knows—"

As if on cue, her grandmother strolled in, with Lawrence Duncan beside her. She smiled and waved at them, but instead of coming over to say hello, she took her date's hand and guided him to the other side of the restaurant and a conspicuously dark corner.

"Maggie obviously wants to be alone with her date tonight," Lion said, humor threading his tone.

"She's going to have problems with that if Bo is coming over."

"Ah." Lion nodded with a new understanding. "Which is probably the whole purpose of having a table that's so private."

"And in a dark corner, which by the way, has never been quite that dark before."

"What did she do? Unscrew a lightbulb?"

"There's no telling." She grinned wryly. "Enjoy the quiet while you can. Tonight could get pretty lively."

"I haven't been bored once since I've been here."

Her grin faded. "I'm afraid it's been a little too lively for you. I can't tell you how much I hate it that your watch has been stolen."

"Don't worry about it."

"Did Bo say he'd found out something?"

"No, not yet."

She shook her head. "Nothing like this has ever happened here before."

"The watch will be found, Gabi, as will the person who took it. And that person *will* pay."

Glints of steel flashed in his eyes, and she stilled. Lion possessed an abundance of charm and magnetism, which often made her forget something very important. First and foremost, Lion was a very hard man.

No matter how easily she joked and laughed with him, even kissed him, it was imperative she remember he was a Damaron, with all the power and money in the world. He *could*, and *would* be completely ruthless to anyone who crossed him or his.

"What is it that's got you thinking so hard?" Lion asked, his voice a velvet rasp.

"I was thinking that I'd never want to be touched by your ruthlessness."

He slowly smiled. "Gabi, you do worry about the strangest things."

A chill shuddered through her. Ray arrived with their wine, then glided away to see to Maggie and Lawrence. Giving herself a few moments to emotionally regroup, Gabi looked away from Lion.

She had a good view of her grandmother, who was flirting and laughing with Lawrence, and of the Koslows, who were toasting their marriage with the champagne Lion had sent over. Both couples were examples of love and its varied complexities, she mused. Her grandmother had had her great love, yet she was still willing and able to play at a new game of love. And the young, earnest Koslows had committed to a love they believed and hoped would last their entire lives. Mentally she saluted all of them.

But as for her and Lion, love wasn't involved, and they would have only tonight together. She took several sips of wine, then without preamble, she broached a subject that would give her a large and much-needed jolt of reality. "When Bo finds your watch, you'll be leaving."

His gaze turned thoughtful. "Sooner or later I'll be leaving, yes."

She nodded. "I imagine too much inactivity is difficult for you."

"I'm certainly not used to inactivity, but then, since I've been here, I haven't really been all that inactive."

"No, not so far." She took another sip of wine. "You know, normally it's very quiet here, especially during the week. Any groups or conventions usually come in on weekends."

His brows lifted. "Are you recommending I should leave by Monday?"

"Oh, no, of course not. I was simply trying to let you know what you could expect in the unlikely event you do decide to stay that long."

He smiled. "That's very kind of you, but I'm pretty good at finding something to entertain me."

Or *someone*, she thought. This trip he had obviously chosen *her* for his entertainment. Next trip it would be someone else. Unwilling to dwell on it, she rushed on to another subject. "So I gather that you work in the family business?"

He nodded. "You and I have that in common."

"I guess, although I think it's pretty safe to say the *scale* of our respective family businesses is vastly different."

"Maybe so, but your family business would win hands down in the charm department."

"Your family business has no charm?" she asked, inexplicably interested by the fact. "None at all?"

"Off the top of my head, I can't think of even a part of it that would come close to equaling the St. Armand's charm."

"What exactly *is* your family business?"

He shrugged. "We're widely diversified. Banking, real estate, electronics, to name a few."

She'd started the subject to divert him, but she'd ended up being engrossed in it. "And is the company public or private?"

"Private. We always keep what is ours."

Out of nowhere, another chill slid down her spine. "I can appreciate that," she said, doing her best to keep her tone light. "You and your cousins don't have to answer to anyone."

"Only ourselves and each other."

"Is answering to your cousins ever a problem?" she asked, curious. "I mean, do you ever have knock-down-drag-out fights with each other?"

He chuckled. "Not since we were kids."

"You did then?"

"Sure. We were normal kids, which meant we could be absolute terrors when we set our minds to it."

She grinned at the idea of him as a young, high-spirited boy, perhaps with grass in his hair and mud on his clothes, after a rough-and-tumble tussle with a cousin. The more she learned about him, the more she wanted to know. "Are all your cousins like you?"

"In what way?"

"Formidable."

He smiled. "There's that word again."

She shrugged. "It accurately describes you, but it's certainly not negative." She didn't mention the other words she also felt described him, such as sexual and virile, to name only a few. "I would imagine you were born with the trait."

He smiled without comment.

Ray arrived with their food and set about serving them, and Gabi felt the familiar tingling warmth on her skin that indicated Lion was studying her. She did her best to cope by chatting with Ray, and as soon as he finished, she was ready with another question for Lion.

"So, are your cousins as formidable as you?" she asked, genuinely wanting to know.

"Let me put it this way—I would never want to go up against any of them, not individually or in any combination."

"In that case, I guess it's a good thing they're on your side."

"Oh, yeah, definitely." He chuckled, then turned his attention to his dinner.

She did the same, but after several minutes she realized she wasn't as hungry as she'd thought. Or more truthfully, she'd rather talk to Lion than eat. "It sounds as if you have a very interesting family."

He looked at her. "I'd much rather you think *I'm* interesting."

She tensed at the sudden sensuality to his tone. It was as if he had just gone on the offensive. But she saw no purpose in denying what was so blatantly obvious. "I think you're probably the most interesting man I've ever met, Lion."

He sat back and slowly shook his head. "I can't always read you, Gabi."

She gave a self-conscious laugh. "That's hard for me to believe."

"Believe it. For instance, there's something I've been wondering about all evening."

The hairs on the back of her neck rose. She put down her fork and gave him her full attention. "Okay, I know I'm going to regret asking, but what the heck? What have you been wondering?"

"How long you were going to try to pretend we didn't kiss this afternoon."

She stared at him. "Is that what you think I've been doing?"

"Haven't you?"

Her brow crinkled as she seriously pondered what he'd said. "Maybe—I'm not sure. Then again, I don't know why you think I should have brought the subject up."

"It's more like I was *hoping* you would, because I was *hoping* you wouldn't be able to deny that something extraordinary happened between us when we kissed."

"I'm not denying anything, Lion."

"Okay, then how about *avoiding*?"

"It would be pretty tough for me to deny *or* avoid it, because it *was* extraordinary," she said as casually as she could manage. "But then again, if I'd thought about it beforehand, I would have expected it. You're obviously a very experienced man."

"You're not dredging up that playboy label again, are you?"

"Absolutely not."

He contemplated her for several moments. "Okay, then experience aside, did you ever consider that what happened between us was just plain old-fashioned chemistry?"

"No." Chemistry implied the reaction of *two* people, but she'd only been aware of her response, not his.

"I even think," he said slowly, seeming to measure each word, "that what happened between us was more involved and more complicated than simple chemistry."

To question him further would leave herself open and vulnerable. Unfortunately, the knowledge couldn't overrule her compulsion to ask. "What do you mean?"

Unexpectedly, he fell silent.

To a certain extent, she'd grown accustomed to the intense way he had of focusing on her. But as each moment passed, his concentration on her increased to the point she feared her skin might actually burn. She reached for her wine and was disappointed to discover the glass empty. Her nerves stretched, frayed. When at last he spoke, she almost gasped with relief.

"I guess it's one of those things that if you have to ask, you wouldn't understand."

His enigmatic answer surprised her, baffled her. But before she could come up with what he might have meant, Lion gave her a smile that was both sweet and comforting. Oddly enough, at that moment sweet and comforting seemed easy and even normal for him.

"It's going to be all right, Gabi. There's nothing at all for you to worry about."

Another strange chill flowed down her spine, but this one was quickly followed by warmth. "I'm puzzled, that's all." A huge understatement, she reflected. Adding to her puzzlement was the dark heat in his eyes that hadn't been there a moment before.

"What in the hell is Maggie doing with that guy?"

She practically jumped out her chair. *Bo.* How in the world had she failed to see him come in? *Lion*, came the instant answer. She glanced over at him and saw he had relaxed back in his seat with a wide grin of amusement. As long as Lion was anywhere near her, she wouldn't be able to see Godzilla, even if he happened to be stomping through Gold Springs. "Gran's just having dinner with him, Bo."

At that moment Maggie laughed louder than she had all evening, loud enough to make Bo scowl. "He must be a real funny guy. Who is he?"

"Lawrence Duncan. He's a guest."

Bo's face cleared. "Now, that's what I call a real happy coincidence. Mr. Duncan is one of the people I need to interview, and I think now is a perfect time."

"Well, no, Bo," she said, shaking her head. "I wouldn't think *now* is a particularly good time."

"Gabi, honey, I don't think I've ever *seen* a better time." He moved off toward Maggie's table, his stride purposeful.

With a grin at Lion, Gabi shrugged. "Stand by. The curtain's going up."

His golden eyes twinkled. "And we've got a front-row seat."

"Yeah, whether we want it or not. And . . . Uh-oh—here comes Gran."

In a clear snit, Maggie yanked a chair up to their table and plopped down. "The *nerve* of that man, interrupting our dinner like that. Can you two believe the absolute gall of Bo? I mean *gall*. And poor Lawrence—well, what could he do? I'm sure he's never run into anyone as rude as Bo. Ray, bring me a glass of wine, will you?" With split-second timing, she threw the order over her shoulder, then continued without missing a beat. "Lawrence is such a gentleman, and he didn't want me upset. To keep the peace, and thinking only of me, Lawrence agreed to give Bo a few minutes. And we were having such a wonderful time too." She finally paused to draw a breath and looked from one to the other. "Well? What do you two think?"

Folding her arms across her waist, Gabi eyed her sternly. "I think the evening is going just as you planned."

Maggie leaned forward, her anger abruptly replaced by a conspiratorial manner. "Do you think Bo was jealous?"

Lion chuckled and Gabi rolled her eyes. "Yes, Gran, he was jealous."

"Marvelous." Maggie practically cackled with glee. "Serves him right too. I happen to know he took Mary Ann Murdock to the movies last week."

"Did you ever think he might be trying to make *you* jealous?"

"Well, the *nerve* of him." Maggie sat back, obviously stunned at the idea.

Gabi looked over at the two men and noticed that Bo appeared dressed for an evening out, rather than work. Or dressed to catch Maggie's attention. But he was every inch the sheriff as he asked questions and took notes. And Lawrence Duncan seemed perfectly at ease and innocent—not that she'd really know what a guilty person would look like. But she was rooting for him and sincerely hoped no one she knew was guilty of the thefts.

She returned her attention to her grandmother. "You should be ashamed of yourself, Gran, using a nice man like Mr. Duncan."

Maggie waved a hand. "Nonsense. Lawrence has been having a great time, and as a matter of fact, so have I. Lion, what do you think? Give me a man's point of view on this. Don't you think Bo's acting like a complete as—

"Oh, hello, Bo. Are you through interrogating my date?"

"For now, but I may need to talk to him again."

"Oh, pu-leeze. You don't have a thing on him and you know it. Anyone with a good pair of eyes can see Lawrence is a refined, sophisticated man who would *never* be capable of doing something as reprehensible as stealing. If you'd just asked me in the first place, I would have told you so."

"As I recall," Bo drawled, "you did tell me. About him and everyone else who is or has ever stayed here, not to mention your entire staff."

"And I'm right too," she said, standing and pointing her finger at him.

"Maggie, darlin', stop worrying and let me do my job."

"I just wish you didn't have to interrogate my friends."

"*Question*, Maggie," Bo said gently. "Not *interrogate*. And you know, don't you, that I wouldn't do it if it wasn't necessary."

The wind seemed to go out of her. She softened and swayed toward him. "Oh, Bo . . ."

"Maggie?" Lawrence strolled up to her. "What do you think of adjourning to the Pump Room for after-dinner drinks and dessert?"

All signs of her softness vanished. "I think it's an absolutely *inspired* idea, Lawrence." She hooked an arm through his and gave Bo an arch look. "You're through, aren't you?"

Bo nodded reluctantly. "Mr. Duncan, you did say you were going to be around for the next few days, didn't you?"

Lawrence smiled down at Maggie. "I have no plans to leave anytime soon."

"Good." Bo watched bleakly as the couple left the restaurant, with Maggie gazing in fascination at Duncan the whole way. "Gabi," he said, "your grandmother has a bad habit of playing with fire."

"Yeah, I know." She grinned at Lion. "Luckily she seems to be fireproof."

"So *far*." He flipped a page of his notebook and read. "Let's see . . . Charles and Letticia Wentworth. They checked in one day before the first theft and are still here. Do you know where they are this evening?"

"I haven't seen them tonight. They must have gone out for dinner."

He made a note. "What are they like?"

She shrugged. "Ordinary tourists."

He shook his head, a wry grin on his craggy face. "I hate to tell you, honey, but ordinary people make the best crooks."

"It can't be them, Bo. They're too nice."

"I wonder where I've heard that before?" He smiled as he closed his notebook. "Okay, I'm going to hang out for a while and talk to a few folks. Hopefully the Wentworths will be back before too long."

She glanced at her watch. "The reunion dinner

will be over in a few minutes, and as soon as the dishes are cleared, the staff who aren't needed for the dance will be getting off. If you want to talk to any of them, that would be a good time."

"Good—I'll watch out for them." Bo nodded at Lion. "I'll be in touch."

"I'd appreciate that." Lion's gaze stayed on Bo's ramrod-straight back until he had left the room.

"Well," Gabi said, "at least there was no bloodshed."

"Not externally, at any rate."

She had a sudden thought. "You know, I'm very surprised you're leaving this investigation entirely in Bo's hands. I would have thought you'd bring in a private army or something."

"It's Bo's jurisdiction. He deserves a chance at it— for one more day." His voice was quiet, matter-of-fact.

"And then what?"

"Then I take over."

She could only imagine what would happen after that. "Can I please just ask that you leave the hotel standing?" she asked, only half kidding.

"I wouldn't hurt you or yours, Gabi. Surely you know that."

No, she didn't, she thought, absorbing the caress of his deep, husky tone. She pushed away her dinner plate. "I'm finished."

He glanced at her barely touched dinner. "Would you like dessert?"

"No, I don't think so. In fact—"

"Forgive us for interrupting." It was Jason Koslow, holding hands with his pretty young wife. "We wanted to personally thank you for the champagne."

"It was our pleasure," Lion said, nodding graciously.

Gabi smiled at the two. "Happy anniversary, and may you have many, many more."

"Thank you, we will." The young man glanced at his wife, then back at them. "Well, thanks again and good night."

"Good night." Humor glinted in Lion's eyes as he looked at Gabi. "For a restaurant that's having a slow night, it's certainly been busy."

"At this table, anyway." She paused. "Actually, I enjoyed having them stop by. I think it's nice to see a couple as happy and in love as they obviously are."

"I agree."

He meant it, she realized, and for a moment was tempted to ask if he believed in marriage and children and white picket fences. But she couldn't envision a fence strong enough to hold him. Most of all, she wasn't up to hearing him say marriage and children were not for him.

His brows arched in query. "Were you about to say something before our latest interruption?"

She nodded, remembering she'd been trying to decide whether or not to bring their evening together to a close. Saying good night now would be the safest route for her to take, but it also would be the dullest. In the end, her desire to spend more time with him easily defeated her good sense. "I was about to ask you if you'd like a cup of coffee or an after-dinner drink."

"I'd like that very much, but not here."

"The Pump Room?"

Holding her gaze, he slowly shook his head. "My suite. I want to be alone with you, Gabi, without any more interruptions."

There it was, she thought—the reason she should have just said good night.

"Well?" he asked.

"You're talking about more than just having coffee in privacy without interruptions, aren't you?"

"Yes, I am."

"And if all I want to do is have coffee?"

"Then that's all we'll do." He stood, tossed several bills onto the table, then took her hand and drew her to her feet. "All you need to do is tell me what you want."

He made it sound so simple, she thought. And it would be *if* she knew what she wanted. He stroked the back of his fingers down the side of her face, and she exhaled a breath she hadn't known she'd been holding. "We can call for the coffee once we get up to your suite."

He tilted her face up and kissed her. It was a long, deep, hot kiss, and when he finished, she was left even more shaken than she'd been after he'd kissed her this afternoon.

"Let's go," he said.

She moved beside him, but she wasn't aware of her feet touching the floor. Her mind raced, but she was unable to think. Heat held her in its grip, and Lion held her attention.

"Mr. Damaron?" Michael called from behind the reception desk. "Wyatt Damaron has been trying to reach you. He asked that you call him as soon as you finished dinner."

Lion nodded. "Thank you."

"Do you think something's happened?" Gabi asked.

"A family emergency, you mean?" He paused long enough to brush a strand of hair off her face. "No, I was expecting the call. There are a couple of things we were supposed to go over. I'll get hold of him and tell him I'll call him back sometime tomorrow." He squeezed her hand. "We've already had enough interruptions this evening."

She saw the elevator up ahead, and then she heard Debra King calling her name. "Gabi?" The beautiful woman rushed up to her, tears welling in her eyes. "Thank *goodness* I found you. My diamond ring is missing, my *engagement* ring."

"Oh, *no*." Gabi's heart sank. This third theft made an already bad situation awful. She glanced at Lion. There was no way she could put Debra off. "What happened, Debra?"

"I'm not sure. I didn't notice I wasn't wearing my ring until dinner was nearly over. I immediately ran up to the room, but it wasn't there." She pressed a hand to her mouth, fighting not to cry.

"When do you last remember seeing it?"

"I went up a little after five to get ready for our

dinner and call home to check on our girls." She spoke slowly, obviously trying hard to concentrate and remember. "I sat on the bed while I talked, and I must have taken off the ring then and laid it on the nightstand." Her voice broke. "Afterward I took a shower."

"But you're not sure about where or when you put down the ring?"

She shook her head, her expression crumbling. "I was upset. Gordon and I had been arguing earlier, and he didn't return to the room until about ten minutes before the dinner started." She gave a soft moan. "He's furious with me, because he thinks I lost the ring on purpose."

"Oh, no, I'm sure he doesn't."

"Oh, yes, I do." Gordon weaved his way up to them, a drink in his hand. "She wants to be single again so she can be with Douglas."

Debra paled and placed a restraining hand on his arm. "Gordon, stop it. You know that's not true."

"The hell it isn't." He waved his glass, and whiskey sloshed over its sides. "They probably know. All our friends know. You've always regretted marrying me. I've *never* been good enough. I just sell cars, but he's a big-time dentist."

"Leave her alone, Gordon," Douglas said, hurrying up to them. "Debra, I just heard what happened. What can I do to help?"

"Oh, look, here's Mr. Big Shot now." Gordon sneered, and more whiskey sloshed as he gestured wildly with the glass. "Get the hell out of here, Dougie Boy. Debra's *my* wife, not yours."

"Gordon, please . . ." Debra attempted to gently pry the drink away from him, but he shrugged her off and finished off the drink with one swallow.

"Enough, guys," Gabi said, holding out her hands. "Try to calm down. Our sheriff is in the hotel, and the sooner we can let him know what happened, the sooner we can find the ring."

"That's a good idea," Debra said. "Gordon, why don't you have a cup of coffee, and I'll go with Gabi to give the sheriff the report."

"Sure, honey. And while I'm drinking coffee the good dentist can comfort you."

"I don't know why she puts up with you, Gordon." Douglas shook his head with disgust. "Deb, you go on, and I'll see that he gets some coffee into him."

Douglas's statement galvanized Gordon. "You *bastard*!" Surprisingly quick for someone so drunk, Gordon threw a punch that connected with the other man's jaw and sent him staggering.

"*Gordon*," Debra cried.

Gabi lunged toward Gordon, but Lion was there before her, stepping between the two men. With breathtaking ease, he thrust Douglas out of the way and took control of Gordon.

"Gabi, you go with Debra and make the report," Lion said quietly. "Douglas, you return to the party. Gordon, you're coming with me to the Pump Room, where you're going to drink an entire pot of coffee."

Gabi smiled at him. "Thank you."

"After I see to him"—he nodded his head toward Gordon, who stood limply in his grip—"I'll go on up and place that call to Wyatt. Come when you can."

She nodded. "Fine."

Lion cut his gaze to Douglas. "Weren't you leaving?"

"Yeah, sure," he said. "Debra—"

"Not another word," Lion said softly.

With a shrug and a last look at Debra, Douglas left.

Gabi placed a hand on Debra's arm. "The report shouldn't take long at all."

Debra eyed her husband uncertainly. "As soon as I'm through, Gordon, I'll come to the Pump Room."

"Do whatever you want," he mumbled. "I don't care anymore."

The tears Debra had been fighting so hard to contain came flooding down her face. "I'm so sorry to cause all this trouble," she told Gabi.

"Don't be," Gabi said reassuringly. "And don't worry, we're going to find your ring."

She sincerely hoped she wasn't wrong. She also sincerely hoped to come to a decision about what she wanted before it was time to go to Lion's suite.

EIGHT

Gabi stared at the door to Lion's suite. It had taken her longer than she would have guessed to finally arrive here, and now that she had, her heart was beating so hard, she couldn't catch her breath. To give herself time to compose herself, she moved a few steps down the hall and leaned against the wall.

She'd stayed with Debra until she had calmed, then she'd checked Gordon. He'd been nursing a cup of coffee in the Pump Room, developing a monumental headache, and, not surprisingly, in no mood to communicate with anyone. Next, she'd gone on an unsuccessful search for her grandmother and had concluded that Maggie, in her continuing effort to get the best of Bo, most likely had suggested a walk or a drive to Lawrence.

No wonder she needed this time to herself, Gabi reflected. Tension, intermittent chaos, and a strong sensual current had filled her evening with Lion. Just being with him had given her a mental workout, sending her through a tangled, complicated range of emotions. He'd fired her imagination as well as her blood, leaving her feeling rushed and confused.

When a crisis had sent them in two different directions, his energy, his heat, his desire had remained with her.

But strangely, during the ensuing tumult, she'd been able to consider all that she knew of him and all that she felt for him. Now her lingering doubts were gone and she knew what she wanted.

She wanted to spend the coming hours with Lion, making love with him and learning his passion.

She still understood that she couldn't take to her heart anything about him—not what he did, or what he might happen to promise in the heat of the moment. And she still understood that soon she'd turn around and find him gone.

But he was here tonight, incredibly virile and sensual, and she wanted him.

She pushed away from the wall and stepped to the door. Lion answered before she had a chance to knock a third time.

"Gabi," Lion said, his voice a whisper.

He wasn't accustomed to dealing with nerves, and it had never occurred to him that a woman could make him feel pain. But tonight, as he'd waited to see whether or not Gabi would show up, he'd learned about nerves and the pain of uncertainty. And it had been hell.

He'd paced and stared at the clock and willed her to come to him, but minutes had ticked by without him hearing from her.

Now he was almost afraid to believe she was finally here. She might be a fabrication of his mind, a vision who would disappear if confronted by the reality of too much force, or even just his normal speaking voice. "I wasn't sure you were coming," he said, again whispering.

"I wasn't either."

Before she could disappear, or change her mind, he reached for her hand and drew her into the parlor. Just looking at her made his throat dry. If possible, she looked even lovelier than she had earlier. The sweater she'd worn for dinner was gone, leaving only green silk, thin straps, and bare, satiny skin. "Any news on Debra's ring?"

"No," she said, moving farther into the room, "but Bo's been told. Oh"—she glanced at him over her shoulder—"and there's a lady named Camilla with the reunion group who's a psychic. She's offered to conduct a séance to try to find out where the ring is."

"A séance?"

"Well, maybe not exactly a séance, but something like that." She reached out to straighten a lampshade. "Seems Camilla has guides who help her out from time to time in cases like this."

"Guides?"

"You know, spirits who give her advice when she asks. Last time I saw her, she was running around the hotel gathering up every candle she could get her hands on and muttering about the importance of creating a receptive mood. I would imagine the séance is going on as we speak." She grinned at him. "And you'll be glad to know I asked her to check on your watch while she was at it."

"Thank you," he said, his gaze on her grin, the first one she'd given him since she'd walked in. "I think."

"Hey, what can it hurt? And who knows? It might even help." She walked around the couch and straightened another lampshade. "Were you able to get hold of your cousin?"

He nodded, wondering why she was straightening already perfectly straight lampshades. Was she nervous? "Our business is all taken care of." He decided not to mention that Wyatt had spent most of the time asking about her. Apparently, the family grapevine had been buzzing. First chance he had, he planned to have a few words with Yasmine about that.

"So you won't have to call him tomorrow?"

"No." Because he so badly wanted to reach for her, he slipped his hands into his pockets. But he strolled toward her, slowly drawing nearer and nearer. "Would you like me to order a fresh pot of coffee?"

She glanced at the coffee service laid out on the table and the one used cup. "No, thank you, but I'm glad you didn't wait for me."

Finally halting in front of her, he was unable to

resist smoothing his fingers along the top of her shoulder. "Would you like something else, then?"

"No, nothing." She looked up at him, her gaze level and direct. "I came here to make love with you, Lion."

Her calmly stated declaration knocked the wind completely out of him. "Are you sure?"

She lifted her arms to encircle his neck. "I don't think I've ever been more sure about anything."

His body took over, tensing, hardening, and his mind shut down. With a groan, he pulled her against him and crushed his mouth to hers, and her lips parted and her tongue thrust upward to meet his. Her taste intoxicated him, her scent bewitched him, the feel of her sent his head reeling.

He cupped the weight of her breast and was electrified when she perfectly filled his hand. He went a little wild then, kneading and caressing the softness, rubbing the silk over her sensitive skin, causing her to murmur and twist in his arms. Then flicking his thumb back and forth, he coerced her nipple to stiffen.

But it wasn't enough for him, not nearly. Frustrated by the material that kept him from her skin, he quickly slid his other hand beneath her skirt to the silky warmth of her thighs.

He knew he was in trouble. The night was young and he'd only begun to kiss her, and touch her, and do all the things he'd been longing to do to her, but already his control was hanging by a thread.

It wasn't like him. With the other women he'd

known intimately, he had always taken his time, drawing out the lovemaking so that they could both experience the pleasure. Yet with Gabi, he wanted all of her all at once, and right now—an impossible feat, he acknowledged.

The fact tormented him. In reality, it would take a lifetime to get his fill of her. And even though she was returning his kisses just as hungrily as he was giving them, he knew he still had to win her heart.

He struggled for control, battling against himself and the passion that kept growing, expanding, deepening inside him. With sheer grit and will, he forced himself to take hold of her arms and tore his mouth from hers. Tonight was their first time, and God help him, for her sake, he wanted it to be special. But when he looked down at her, he nearly changed his mind.

"What's wrong?" she asked, her large brown eyes filled with confusion and luminous desire.

He drew in a ragged breath that felt as if it cut its way out of his chest. "I need to slow down."

"Why?" she asked, all seduction now and alluring temptress. One by one, she began to undo the buttons of his shirt. "Are you tired?"

His insides quivered with the turbulent force of his need for her, while she was relaxed and confident. It took him a second to realize she was actually teasing him. "No," he said, his voice a rough growl, "but as tough as it is to keep up with you, I sure as hell should be."

She laughed softly, bewitchingly. "You don't have

to slow down for me, Lion. I *want* you to make love to me."

He traced an unsteady finger over her lips, already slightly swollen from his hard kisses. "Be careful what you say, Gabi. I'm already on the edge."

With his shirt opened to the waist, her fingers made a trail through the dark gold hair that covered the width of his chest. "I wouldn't have come up here if I didn't want you to go over that edge and take me with you."

Using one hand, he gripped both of hers, stopping her before her tantalizing touches drove him completely out of his mind. "Where did you learn to do that?"

She smiled. "I looked at you and just knew."

He slowly shook his head in wonder. "You don't know what you're doing."

"Maybe not, but I want to find out."

He shoved his fingers through her hair, then fiercely clenched them. "Don't ever say I didn't try to warn you."

"I won't."

He swept her off her feet into his arms and carried her into the bedroom.

He should be gentle, he thought feverishly as he lowered her to the bed and began to undress her. But his heart was hammering, and his body was throbbing with hunger, and his sanity was nearly gone. She arched against him, making it easier for him to unzip her dress. Like gift wrapping, the silk parted, the straps slid off her shoulders, and the bodice loosened from her body. The sight stunned him.

But she gave him no time to catch his breath. With an eagerness that sent quakes shuddering through him, she yanked his shirt from his pants, then set to work on his belt buckle.

Need climbed in him, clawed at him, made him clumsy. He tried to help her with his clothes, but he ended up cursing his sudden awkwardness. His fingers were like thumbs, and his grip kept slipping. Wrenching away from her, he sat up to finish the job. As he tossed the last of his clothes away, he felt her hand glide up his spine.

He turned back to her, and his stomach contracted.

Beneath the lamplight, her naked skin gleamed with luminescence, and her hair shone with life as it spread over the pillow. The nipples of her firm breasts were budded and her long legs were slightly parted. "You're the most beautiful thing I've ever seen," he said, his voice hoarse with desire.

A lovely smile curved her lips and she reached up to him. "I feel the same way about you."

His heart gave a hard thud against his rib cage. Time slowed to a crawl. His limbs grew heavy, his every movement became measured, unhurried. Yet contradictorily his need to have her became more urgent.

He bent his head to her mouth, tasting her once again. "I used to have patience," he murmured, his lips moving against hers.

"I've never had patience," she whispered.

With a husky laugh, he kissed the length of her throat to the tender underside of her breast and heard her gasp. Her responsiveness startled him, beguiled him, but most of all, deeply satisfied him. He laved his tongue around her nipple, took the nub between his teeth, and lightly nibbled until he heard her moan, then he suckled until she began to writhe.

"I can't believe I was able to keep my hands off you as long as I did." He was talking to her, to himself, to no one at all.

"What *were* you thinking?" Her breath caught in her throat as his mouth came down on her other nipple.

"I wasn't thinking at all," he murmured, forming his words around the tortured peak, his breath fanning warmly over her skin.

"Lion."

She'd spoken so softly, the sound of his name barely reached him. He lifted his head to look at her, and her image burned into his mind. Heightened color blushed her cheeks and her throat, fire glimmered in her heavily lashed eyes, and her heart beat against his chest in time with his own.

Everything about her hit him on a gut level. She breathed out and she breathed in and he was enthralled. She smiled, she laughed, and inside him, hard-core desire mixed with magical sensations. With a violent shock he realized he not only loved her, he needed her the way he needed to breathe.

Her hands carried a tremor as they lifted to frame

his face. "Can you believe I actually thought I could spend time with you without wanting to make love with you?"

"What *were* you thinking?" he said, repeating her words back to her and making her laugh, as he had hoped. He opened his mouth over hers and swallowed a portion of her laugh. "You should have asked me. I would have told you that you couldn't."

There wasn't a part of him that didn't hurt with hunger for her, but strangely, remarkably, the urgency to have her had eased somewhat.

He skimmed his hand to the flat stretch of skin below her waist, then pressed his lips to the center of her belly. Her hips lifted and undulated, and she moaned again. He needed no further encouragement. His breath teased through the triangle of hair at the apex of her legs, then he probed lower to discover moistness and heat and wonderfully sensitive places to touch and rub.

Her fingers dug into his back, her head turned from side to side. *"Lion."*

The knowledge that he affected her as much as she affected him blazed a path of happiness through him, and his urgency returned, slamming through him with a devastating force, scorching along his nerve endings. He had to fully possess her and he had to do it now.

He quickly fitted himself with protection, then positioned himself between her thighs and entered her. She was small, tight around him, and after a moment he hesitated.

"Don't stop," she whispered, her hands pushing downward on his hips.

The sound of his heartbeat thundered in his ears, heat constricted his lungs. Clenching his teeth until they ached, he set a deliberately slow pace. She rewarded him with murmurs of pleasure and a shower of sweet, hot kisses all over his face. And little by little her body adjusted to his and accepted his length and bulk into her hot silken depths.

But the effort of holding back had taken a ferocious toll on him, and when at last he was completely buried inside her, he jerked back his hips and, using all his pent-up power, thrust deeply into her, melding them into one.

Sensations exploded throughout his body and fire scalded his insides, shocking him, overwhelming him. He drove into her again and again, thrusting deeper and ever harder.

The intensity of his passion made him blind and deaf and the rest of the world ceased to exist. For him, there was only her, and he was utterly relentless with her, his appetite insatiable. He made impossible demands on her, refusing to let her relax or hide any part of her from him.

And she made everything possible, accepting his demands and in return giving him hers. Gripping him tightly, she embraced his power and force and asked him for even more.

He was positive he was going to shatter at any moment, but when he did, he wanted her to be with him. Somehow he waited as she filled his ears with

her murmured words of excitement, of desire, and
took him to a higher plane of ecstasy with her soft,
heated body than he'd ever been to before.

Pleasure coiled, built, became unendurable, un-
bearable. He heard her sobs, felt her hands clutch at
him, and then suddenly she stiffened beneath him and
her inner muscles began to squeeze and contract. A
hard shudder ripped through him as his control finally
broke apart, and he hurtled over the fiery edge of the
world, taking her with him, as she'd said she wanted,
as he'd wanted, as he'd almost destroyed himself
to do.

Cool midnight air flowed through the open bedroom windows, rippling the curtains, dancing lightly
over Gabi's skin, then swirling on to Lion, who lay
beside her. A love song followed the breeze into the
room, its melody a ribbon intended to tie together all
lovers who heard it.

Utterly content, Gabi soaked up the romance of
the moment and all the moments that had just passed.
Lion's arm was a pleasurable weight, lying across her
abdomen, and the heat his body radiated to hers was
comforting. She could hear his steady, even breathing, and knew that he was watching her, his golden
gaze exerting its own unique pressure on her skin.

But she didn't move or turn toward him. His lovemaking had left her boneless, shimmering with
warmth and satisfaction, and she wanted the feeling
and the memories to last as long as possible.

Everything he was as a man had been wrapped up in the way he had made love to her. His power and strong sensuality had been there for her to see, to feel.

She'd been so sure of herself when she'd met him, so safe in her little world. Thankfully, she'd pushed past her pre-conceptions and had gotten to know him, and along the way, she'd discovered how easy and fun it was to be with him. To her surprise it still was.

While they'd made love, something momentous had happened to her. The planets had shifted, and when it was all over, Lion had become the center of her universe.

It was more than possible she had even fallen a little in love with him, though she had no intention of burdening him with that knowledge. Later, after he was gone, she'd deal with her feelings alone. Their remaining time together was too precious to spoil with the sadness she'd surely feel. As if affirming her decision, laughter floated through the window and another love song began to play.

He stirred beside her, and his big hand spread open on her belly, pleasingly possessive. "Sounds like they're having a good time, doesn't it?"

"Uh-huh. They'll probably party all night."

"They'll be tired tomorrow."

"Yeah, but it may be a long time before they see each other again, if at all, and they probably figure they should take advantage of the weekend and rest later." It was a philosophy she planned to take to heart. She would enjoy him now, while she could, and she would rest after he was gone.

His fingers shifted restlessly back and forth over her skin. "How are you feeling?"

"Oh . . . I feel mildly satisfied."

"Mildly satisfied?"

A laugh burbled up out of her. "I can't believe you even had to ask."

With a mock growl, he came up on one elbow. "You're laughing at me again."

"No, no, I'm really not."

He grinned down at her. "Yes, you really are."

She giggled. "You're right—I am."

His grin lingered as he slowly shook his head. "I make love to you and what do you do? You *laugh* at me. That's not a real confidence booster, Gabi."

"I've never known anyone less in need of a confidence booster." Genuinely entertained by the notion that he would be insecure about anything, she laughed again.

He stroked a strand of hair off her forehead. "With you, Gabriela St. Armand, I need all the confidence I can get."

She didn't believe him, of course, but she did her best to wipe all traces of her amusement off her face. "So let me get this straight. You're saying you would prefer it if I regarded our lovemaking in a more serious light?"

His expression was drawn in solemn lines, but his eyes spoiled the effect by glittering with mirth. "Ummm, I'm not sure *serious* is exactly the right word. No—actually, now that I think about it, I would prefer a word more along the lines of *worshipful.*"

"*Ha*—you *wish.*"

His laughter erupted into the air around them. "No?"

"Not a chance, Mr. Damaron. However . . ."

"However?"

"Would it improve your mood if I admitted that I feel *somewhat* better than just mildly satisfied."

"Not really, but *this* will," he said, and brought his mouth down on hers.

She responded with a passion she wouldn't have thought possible a day ago. Kissing him now seemed as natural as if she'd been doing it all her life, and she knew when they made love again, it would be with the same ease. Already, she could feel herself softening in anticipation. He had imprinted her body with a thorough, unforgettable knowledge of his that would stay with her the rest of her life.

Gradually he brought the kiss to an end and lifted away from her. Male arrogance pervaded his expression, along with the saving grace of humor. "*Now* tell me how you feel."

Heat lingered in her veins and sizzled over her skin, but she couldn't resist teasing him again. "Let me think. . . ."

"*What* am I going to do with you?"

"I have a few suggestions." Laughter and desire mingled in her voice as she shifted to cuddle against him and slip an arm around his neck.

"Only a few?"

"Well . . ."

A knock sounded at the parlor door in the next room.

Her head fell back to the pillow. "Oh, no . . ."

"Ignore it," he said gruffly, pulling her back to him. "Whoever it is will go away."

The knock came again.

"I can't ignore it. I'd like to, but I can't." Her tone was regretful, but firm. "Someone may need me."

"*I* need you. And anyway, who would know to look for you here?"

"Anyone with two eyes, I would imagine. And Ray did deliver coffee for two to this room." A golden-brown stubble shadowed his face, drawing her fingers upward to skim along his jaw.

More knocks sounded.

"I'm sorry," she whispered. "I promise I'll come right back if it's not important."

"Never mind," he said with a groan, and slipped off the bed. "I'll get it."

The sight of his nakedness anchored her to the bed, thwarting her intention to also get up. She'd already learned his body by touch, by taste, and now she couldn't resist the opportunity to learn him visually.

As he quickly reached for his slacks and put them on, she watched with admiration, and not for the first time, she was reminded of a big, sleek animal. His muscles flowed beneath his skin, his buttocks were firm, his thighs were rock hard, and his stomach was ridged. Foolishly, she wished for a sculpture of him.

Even more foolishly, she wished she could ask him to come back to bed.

He shrugged into a shirt, but left it open. "I'll be right back. Don't move."

"I wouldn't think of it." With a grin, she fluffed the pillows behind her and made herself more comfortable. Downstairs the music had heated up again and the percussion of the bass thumped against the walls.

She didn't hear Lion open the parlor door, but she had no trouble hearing what he said.

"Maggie."

NINE

With a silent groan, Gabi slid down in the bed and pulled the sheet up to her neck.

"Hey, handsome," she heard her grandmother say to Lion. "Do you have my granddaughter in here somewhere?"

Gabi pulled the sheet up to her nose.

"Maggie— *Wait*, Maggie. Where are you going?"

"Why, to see my granddaughter, of course. I'm assuming she's in the bedroom? *Yoo-hoo, Gabi.*" Her voice grew louder as she drew closer. "Are you in there, darling?"

Feeling dread and an odd sort of fascination, Gabi stared at the doorway. There was no use asking how her grandmother had tracked her down. When she set her mind to it, there was nothing she couldn't find out. She compelled, coerced, bribed, and flirted, but most of all she used her intuition.

Maggie strolled into the room, a bright smile on

her face, a tray of milk and cookies in her hand. "Ah, *there* you are, darling. And what perfect timing I have. It looks as if you and Lion could use a little nutrition break."

"Hi, Gran." Accepting the inevitable, she pushed herself upright, bringing the sheet with her.

Maggie took a seat on the opposite side of the bed from Gabi and placed the tray between them. "I've brought your favorite—white-chocolate-and-pecan cookies."

"So you have. I also notice you brought *three* glasses of milk. You must be planning to stay awhile."

Maggie held out a glass of milk to Lion, who declined with a shake of his head. "Pull up a chair, Lion. Make yourself comfortable."

"Thanks, but I'm fine." He moved off to the bathroom.

Gabi snagged a cookie, took a bite, then used the remainder to gesture at her grandmother. "I'm always happy to see you, Gran, you know that. But in this particular instance, I can't help wondering why you're here."

"Don't I always bring you milk and cookies when you're having trouble sleeping?"

"Uh-huh. And on those very rare occasions, you *know* I'm having trouble sleeping because I call and tell you—something I didn't do tonight."

Maggie shrugged. "You were busy."

Lion reappeared with a St. Armand bathrobe and tossed it across the bed to Gabi. She kept the sheet against her until she'd shrugged into the robe and tied it around her waist. "Okay, Gran, what's wrong? Most of the time when you bring me milk and cookies, it's because *you* can't sleep. So why can't you sleep tonight?"

Maggie chose a cookie, then, with a grim and worried expression, set about picking out all the pecans. "I heard about Debra King's ring."

"That's what I thought. I'm sorry, Gran. I gather the ring hasn't been found yet."

"No, and Bo hasn't been able to come up with anything that might help either."

"Is he still here?"

"He left a little while ago, but he'll be back in the morning."

Gabi glanced at Lion, who had one hip propped on the windowsill. She imagined this was a first for him, having the grandmother of the woman with whom he'd just made love barge right into his bedroom. But he seemed to be taking it well. "Try a cookie, Lion. They're wonderful."

"No, thanks," he said, and smiled at her.

Warmth fluttered in her stomach. Yes, she thought. She was probably in love with him.

Maggie picked up the plate of cookies and held it out to him. "For goodness' sake, have a cookie. It'll give you energy, and a few sips of milk wouldn't hurt you either. Calcium makes things stiff."

"*Gran.*"

Her eyes were wide with innocence. "Well, it does, darling. Everyone knows that. Nothing's better for your bones than calcium."

"I surrender." Grinning wryly, Lion helped himself to a glass of milk and a couple of the cookies, then returned to his position at the window.

Maggie gave him an approving look. "Don't worry, I'll be leaving soon."

"You're welcome to stay as long as you want, Maggie."

More warmth moved through Gabi, along with gratitude to him for his forbearance. She doubted there were many men who, under the circumstances, would show the same consideration. In fact, he had just eliminated the *probably* from her mind, she realized. She *was* in love with him.

Maggie started pulling pecans out of another cookie. "Bo did say he'd managed to talk to quite a few of the people on his list tonight, including all the staff who normally have access to the rooms. Thank goodness he seems to have decided they're innocent. Of course, I'd already told him they were."

"Do you know if he has plans to question anyone else?"

Maggie grimaced. "Oh, yes—the rest of the employees. He says locks can be picked, copies of keys made, anything. And then there's Lawrence and the Wentworths, who were here when the first item disappeared." She sternly surveyed the cookie for any remaining pecans, then took a nibble. "At least the party is going well. Oh, but I saw Gordon King heading up to his room, looking extremely unwell. I hope he's not coming down with something."

"He is—a hangover the size of Canada."

"I'm glad you told me. I'll have a batch of Uncle Marvin's hangover cure sent up to him."

"I'd rather you let him suffer a little longer. He was horrible to poor Debra."

"Oh? Well, then that's perfect. Before Uncle Marvin's cure will make him better, it'll make him think he's dying."

"Remind me not to cross you two," Lion drawled.

"A valuable lesson to learn early," Maggie said.

Laughter played around the corner of his mouth. "Should I even ask what happened to your date?"

"Nothing dire," she said with a shrug. "We went for a walk after dinner, then I left him in the lobby, whole and in one piece. I told him I had some work to do."

"Wanted to ditch him, huh?"

"Yeah, pretty much." She reached for another cookie. "Oh, and Gabi, I saw the Wentworths come in. Such a nice couple. They'd gone out to dinner, but Bo was able to have a word with them before they went upstairs." She paused. "Bo looked handsome tonight, didn't you think, Gabi?"

"He looked *very* handsome," she said, throwing a quick grin at Lion. "Any idea how long you'll continue waging your silly war against him?"

Maggie rubbed tiredly at her eyes. "Well, now that you mention it, I am getting a little bored with the whole thing."

"Uh-huh. And so?"

"Actually . . ." Maggie studied the remaining cookies. "I'm thinking about letting him win."

"Why, what a *good* idea, Gran."

She pushed herself up from the bed. "Yeah, well, I'll see how I'm feeling in the morning. After some sleep, I may think of an entirely new battle campaign."

Lion chuckled. "Rest well, Maggie."

"I will." She paused in the bedroom doorway, her expression pure mischief. "But I hope you two don't get a wink of sleep."

"Good night, Gran," Gabi said firmly.

With a thumbs-up signal, Maggie was gone.

As if nothing extraordinary had happened, Lion moved the tray Maggie had left behind to the bedside table, then sat down beside her. "I gather she doesn't like pecans."

"She loves them, but she was very upset. And by the way, thank you for being so nice to her."

"No thanks are necessary. I like your grandmother."

"The feeling is mutual, just in case you haven't been paying attention. She's crazy about you."

"Maggie's a wise woman."

"I can see how you'd feel that way," she said with a laugh. "But you really shouldn't be quite so pleased. As with everything involving Gran, the fact that she likes you is not as simple as it might seem on the surface."

"Oh, yeah?" He lifted her hand and pressed his lips to her palm.

Warmth shuddered through her, reminding her of

other, more powerful sensations that had flooded her body as they had made love.

"So what's beneath the surface?" he asked.

She'd been referring to her grandmother's "one great love" theory, veiled though she had kept the reference. She knew if she told him about the theory, he would either pack his bags and leave immediately, or he would become hysterical with laughter. Neither reaction would make her happy. So why had she even brought it up?

"Gabi? What's beneath the surface?"

She had a quick debate with herself, then let out a quiet breath. "Well, Gran believes there's one great love in every woman's life, and she's decided that you are mine."

He didn't laugh *or* flinch, but he also gave nothing away. "I gather you don't agree?"

A truthful answer would reveal much more to him than she was willing to reveal. Now that she'd brought the theory up, the only thing she could do was make light of it. She rolled toward him and threw one bare leg over his. "Don't be afraid," she said, her voice low and throaty, her fingers provocative and teasing as they traced the angle of his jaw.

"I'm not. Did you really think I would be?"

She doubted if anything would scare him, but she'd said the first thing that had popped into her head. In retrospect, she should have waited for the second thing. Lion would be accustomed to women falling in love with him, and he wouldn't be frightened away at the first hint of the word *love*. And she couldn't think of anything that had ever annoyed her more.

Determined to give him a least a few uncomfortable moments, she snuggled closer and infused her voice with playful menace. "You *should* be afraid. You should be *very* afraid."

"And why's that?" he asked, clearly amused.

"Well, because . . . What if I believed the way Gran does? What if I decided you *were* the love of my life, and I became *obsessed* with you?"

"Ah, I see what you mean. Ummm . . . This is going to require some thinking." He slid his hand beneath her and rubbed her soft bottom.

She lightly pushed at his shoulder. "What are you doing?"

"I'm thinking."

She laughed. "You're *stalling*. Give me an answer."

"Okay, okay." He chuckled. "Well, it's like this, Gabi. You're completely amazing when you're *not* obsessed with me, so . . . I'd have to conclude that if you *were*, you'd be nothing short of a full-fledged miracle."

This wasn't going as she'd expected or wanted. Aggravated, she tapped the tip of her finger against his chin. "You're not taking this seriously. *Think* about it, Lion. What if when you leave here, I came after you? What if I began to *stalk* you?"

"Stalk me?" He closed his hand around her tapping finger. "You mean you'd do stuff like hide in the bushes around my house and go through my trash?"

"I wouldn't go through trash for anyone," she said

firmly, "but I might consider lurking in your bushes if the leaves aren't too pointed."

"I'll immediately replant with stalker-friendly bushes."

She broke away from him and leaned back against the pillows. "You're still not taking me seriously, Lion, but you should. If I decided to, I could be very good at stalking. You wouldn't be able to make a move without me knowing, and I'd . . . I'd . . . Well, I don't know exactly what all I'd do, but trust me, I would make your life a living hell." This last idea appealed to her.

With an enormous laugh, he shifted onto his side and pulled her against his hard body. "Gabi, you can follow me, you can monitor my every move, you can tap my phone, you can even try lurking in my bushes. But if I were you, I wouldn't go to all that trouble. All you'd have to do is ring my doorbell and tell me you want to come in. Or even easier, pick up the phone and call me to come get you."

"And you would?"

He grinned. "So fast it would make your beautiful head spin."

Her head was already spinning and her heart was somersaulting. "You will forget me, you know," she said softly and seriously.

"Not on the longest day of my life," he said, equally soft, equally serious.

Her blood thickened and heated, and she pressed two fingers to his lips. "For a playboy," she whispered, "you say the nicest things."

"Have I ever told you that you scare me to death?" he asked, his eyes a dark gold.

"No." She didn't believe him, but at that moment it didn't matter.

"It's true. I never know what to expect from you." He scraped the pads of her fingers along the edge of his teeth. "If you don't end up giving me heart failure, you'll most certainly drive me crazy."

"Hush, now," she whispered, "we've talked long enough." She drew her fingers away and replaced them with her mouth and tongue.

He pushed the robe off her shoulder, and kneaded his hand down her body to the curve of her hips. The heat began to rise in her, and the desire began to grow. This lovemaking, she sensed, would be different from the last. And she was right.

This time he didn't explore her, he devoured her. This time his teeth bit more than nibbled, and his tongue scraped more than stroked. He gasped for air more than he breathed, and she didn't think she breathed at all.

The sweetness burned through her, the intimacy went beyond her comprehension. The sensations were darker, more potent. She caught fire and shivered. She demanded, and he showed her no mercy.

The music seemed to grow louder, the night hotter. He made her his when she already was his. And when the orgasm came, it came in gigantic waves, rolling over her, pounding through her, leaving her scorched, spent, trembling. And even more in love with him than she had been before.

❦━━━━━❦

Gabi leaned against the windowsill. Behind her, the dawn sky was lightening to a pearlized gray and the animals in the woods were beginning to stir, but her gaze was on Lion as he slept, his powerful body relaxed. He'd drawn a sheet up to his waist, but one muscled leg had escaped to lie on top. He had one arm crooked above his head, the other rested across his middle.

The night had been beyond anything she'd ever known or expected. Heat remained in her body, his scent covered her skin, and memories of the things they had done filled her mind.

She'd awakened after only a couple of hours of sleep, unwilling to waste any of the time they had left together. She'd much rather be laughing with him, or making love with him, or even simply watching him, as she was doing now.

But with every moment that passed, she was finding it harder and harder to hide her love from him.

She'd blundered when she'd told him about her grandmother's theory. She could have easily ended up revealing more than she'd intended. Looking back, she realized she'd been testing his reaction, hoping he might disclose some of his deeper feelings. He hadn't, of course.

A slight smile touched her lips. She wouldn't make a mistake like that again. When he left, she wanted no tears, no recriminations, no bad feelings.

She turned and saw the sky had lightened. Two

deer had ventured out to graze on the lawn. A rabbit sat at the edge of the woods, surveying them. And a raccoon, Rocky, if she wasn't mistaken, was scurrying toward the hotel, no doubt on his way to the kitchen door to see if he could get a handout.

"Good morning," Lion murmured, his mouth close to her ear, his strong hands circling her waist.

"I didn't hear you get up." She relaxed back against him. "You move very quietly."

"Apparently so do you. You slipped out of bed without me knowing it."

"There was no need for both of us to be awake."

He pressed a kiss to the side of her neck. "I can think of *one* excellent reason."

She laughed softly. "Well, there is that. But I knew you'd wake up soon. You don't seem like the kind of man who would need a lot of sleep."

He gave a playful growl. "You think you've got me pretty much figured out, don't you?"

"Uh-huh," she said, lying.

"Boy, do I have some surprises for you."

"That's good," she said, shifting around in his arms and sliding her hands behind his neck. "I *like* surprises."

"Do you?" He smiled, but his expression was thoughtful. "We'll see."

"When?"

"Probably sooner than you're ready."

"That sounds very ominous."

"I hope not." Suddenly he laughed. "You know what? I'm hungry."

She tilted her head, mildly curious to know what he'd been talking about, but after a moment she decided he must have been joking with her. "The milk and cookies didn't stick with you, huh?"

"Nope. How early does the kitchen serve breakfast?"

"On Sundays, a buffet starts at seven in the restaurant, but this morning, there'll also be a brunch in the ballroom at ten for the reunion group."

"Are you scheduled to work?"

"No, but I should probably check on things in a little while."

He smiled. "I don't think you're going to have time."

She chuckled. "Oh, really?"

"Really." His gaze lifted to the scene beyond the window. "There's a raccoon racing toward the woods."

"It's probably Rocky. I saw him earlier. I'm sure someone in the kitchen gave him some food and now he's off to wash it in the creek."

"He's a busy little guy." He looked down at her. "In fact, just watching him is making me tired. Why don't we go back to bed?"

Her pulses quickened. "I thought you were hungry."

"Right now I have a different kind of appetite that needs feeding."

"That's good—that's *very* good—because so do I." She took his hand and drew him toward the bed.

As the elevator descended to the lobby Gabi enviously eyed Lion's crisp appearance. He looked as rested as if he'd had a full night's sleep. "Do you realize it's already ten-thirty?"

"Is it?" He smiled at her with complete unconcern.

"Yes." She'd managed to make it down the back stairway to her room without being detected, but the outfit she'd changed into had gotten wrinkled when she'd returned to Lion's suite and they had made love again. "Maybe I'll get lucky and Gran won't be in the lobby."

"You think she'll give us a bad time because we're so late coming down?"

She grinned. "She'll start with that."

At the first floor, the doors opened onto an almost empty lobby. Michael was on bellman duty, but he was spending the lull watering the plants, Gabi saw as she moved out of the elevator. Mr. and Mrs. Wentworth were in the sitting room, reading the morning paper. And as Gabi had expected, her grandmother was behind the reception desk, waiting for them.

"Good morning, you two," Maggie called out cheerily. "I've been wondering when you were going to manage to get out of bed."

Gabi shot an I-told-you-so look at Lion.

He grinned. "I'm afraid the time just got away from us, Maggie."

"Good for you." She slapped the top of the desk

in delight. "For a while I was thinking of sending up a survival package—you know, champagne, chocolates, the *essentials*—but I finally decided if you needed help, you could call 911, and until then, I should leave you alone."

"That was very considerate of you."

"Not to mention unusual," Gabi added dryly.

Her remark drew Maggie's attention from Lion to her. "Sweetheart, you're positively *glowing* this morning."

"Oh, good. That new moisturizer I bought the other day must really be working."

"Or something *else* is," Maggie said, her tone heavy with meaning.

"Her skin *is* very soft," Lion said. "I can vouch for that."

Gabi rolled her eyes. "Thank you for that testimonial, Lion. It was very helpful." She took his hand and began tugging him away from the desk. "Let's go. If I don't get some coffee in me in the next sixty seconds, I won't be responsible for my actions."

Maggie frowned. "Oh, no, wait. I want to talk to you, darling."

She was sure she did, Gabi thought ruefully. "Later, Gran. Lion and I are starving." Her grandmother wanted her to tell her she'd been right about Lion being the love of her life. Eventually, of course, she would. But right now she simply wasn't ready to face the reality of what it meant to love a man like Lion, a man who would never allow himself to be enclosed by a white picket fence, marriage, and family.

"Then right after you eat," Maggie called after them.

She gave a vague nod and managed to get halfway across the lobby with Lion, when he stopped, forcing her to do the same.

"Gabi, if you want to go back and talk to your grandmother, I'll go on to the restaurant."

"I don't." With a pull, she started him moving again.

"But it might be important."

"She would have said if it was. At any rate, I'll get together with her later." *Much* later, she thought.

"Gabi," he said, when they reached the restaurant doorway. "There's something you should know."

She looked up at him. "What?"

"You don't ever have to pull me. I'm more than willing to go anywhere you want."

If only that were true, she reflected, and found herself entangled in the glittering warmth in his golden eyes. Exhaling a shaky breath, she looked away. "Doesn't that coffee smell heavenly? And the food too. Come on, let's go help ourselves."

She led the way, but this time she deliberately refrained from taking his hand. And she admitted to herself that she'd highly overrated her ability to ignore the bottomless hole his departure would leave in her heart and in her life.

TEN

"Gabi, Lion." Bo nodded to them. "Would you two mind if I join you for a few minutes?"

"Not at all." Lion gestured to one of the vacant chairs at their table.

"Morning, Bo," Gabi said, feeling considerably better than she had when they'd first come into the restaurant. The food and coffee had helped restore her energy, and she'd been able to restore a portion of her good mood by telling Lion a few of the funniest stories about Gold Springs. And somewhere along the line, she'd also managed to gain a renewed strength. When the time came for Lion to leave, she might not be in one piece, but she knew she would survive.

As for Lion, he had listened to her stories with the same concentrated attention he always gave her, but she had sensed that he was trying to work out something of his own, perhaps trying to come to some sort of decision, maybe even about when he would be returning home.

"I'll be interviewing more folks this morning," Bo said, settled in a chair between the two of them. "And I was wondering if either of you'd had any ideas that might possibly help."

Regretfully Gabi shook her head. "I wish I had."

"I do too." Lion took a swallow of his coffee. "You haven't come up with so much as a clue yet?"

Gabi knew Lion well enough now not to be fooled by the softness of his voice. A little support in Bo's direction would not be remiss, she decided. "It's obviously a very hard case."

Bo grimaced. "You've got that right. So far I've come up with a big, fat zero. Whoever's doing this is a stone-cold professional. I've even checked the data banks for similar reports and haven't found a one." He shook his head. "I plan to go back into the computer later this afternoon and make a more detailed search."

Lion put down the cup and eyed the other man levelly. "I'm going to bring you in some help."

Bo froze, and Gabi instinctively tried to smooth over the tension between the two men. "You can appreciate his concern, can't you, Bo?"

Bo's professionalism showed as he successfully kept any umbrage he might have felt to himself. "Lion, I understand how my lack of progress would be troubling to you—"

"I've gone *way* beyond troubled. With every day

my grandfather's watch is gone, the odds increase that it won't be found."

"That's true," Bo said, his gaze never once wavering from Lion's. "And I realize how hard it must be for you to sit by and do nothing, but I need you to continue doing just that. Bringing in outsiders to a small place like Gold Springs is only going to muddy the waters and make my job that much harder."

"I don't see it that way."

"Be that as it may, I'm *still* asking you to hold off on bringing in anyone from the outside."

Gabi put her hand over Lion's. "You can do that, can't you?"

"I'm not sure." His gaze swept to her, then returned to Bo without once softening, but he flipped his hand over and his fingers closed around hers. "For how long, Bo?"

"I can't say exactly, but it shouldn't be too much longer."

"That's extremely vague."

"I know and I'm sorry."

Gabi abandoned her efforts to run interference. Bo was both a sheriff and an ex-marine, which she supposed gave him better odds than most of holding his own with Lion.

Lion leaned back in his chair. "I haven't heard anyone mention the two men who were working at the back of the house yesterday."

"Bill and Mike," Gabi said in explanation to Bo.

"It's not them," he said definitely. "You couldn't find two more honest men anywhere."

Lion was silent for several moments, and when he finally spoke, it was slowly and with great deliberation. "None of you—not you, Bo—not you, Gabi—and certainly not Maggie—want to believe that anyone around here could be guilty. But one of them is very *much* guilty. So if you don't want me bringing in outsiders, I *strongly* suggest that each of you needs to look at this hotel and the people in and around it with a completely fresh eye."

Bo nodded somberly. "You're right."

Gabi remained quiet. Knowing Lion was right didn't make it easier for her to think someone she knew, even casually, was a thief. But her low spirits lifted somewhat when she saw Lion's gaze gradually soften on her.

"There's Maggie," Bo murmured, motioning for her to join them. "She needs to be in on this."

Maggie strolled up to them. "I guess I don't have to ask why the three of you look so serious, do I?"

"We've been discussing the thefts, Gran."

She nodded and took the chair Bo had reached over and pulled out for her. "I didn't see you come in, Bo."

"You were talking with Lawrence Duncan, so I decided not to bother you."

"I see." She cast a glance around the table. "So what's up?"

Needing more caffeine, Gabi drew her hand from Lion's and reached for her coffee cup. "Lion believes that you, Bo, and I need to be more *objective* about the thefts and the people around us."

"I suppose it couldn't hurt," Maggie said guardedly.

"You know he's right, Gran."

Lion looked at her, then turned his attention to Maggie. "I also asked about the two men who were working at the back of the hotel yesterday afternoon."

Maggie shook her head. "Bill and Mike would never steal from me—or anyone else, for that matter. *Never.*"

"So I've been told," he said dryly. "Okay, Maggie, forget about guilt or innocence for now. Tell me what they were working on."

"They were replacing the windows in two of the rooms."

Gabi grinned. "Gran hit a baseball through one of the windows a couple of weeks ago."

"It was really the pitcher's fault," Maggie said with a shrug. "He threw it wide of the plate."

"The pitcher was a nine-year-old guest," Gabi added with wry humor, "and the plate was an upside-down china plate."

"*Not* that it really matters." Maggie sent a sharp look at her granddaughter. "We'd been planning to renovate that bedroom anyway, and the one beside it."

Bo leaned toward her. "You made a heck of a hit. I saw the window the next day. The entire bottom section was shattered."

Maggie gave him a beaming smile. "It really *was* a good hit, wasn't it?"

"Sure was."

"So *have* those rooms been renovated?" Lion asked her.

"Not yet, but the new windows are the start." She brightened as she remembered. "Bill and Mike did such a wonderfully clever job. Lion, you'll appreciate this. They installed a new type of insulated glass into the old frames. That way, the windows still match the others and we don't have to rush to install the new glass in the rest of the windows."

"You strayed off the subject, Gran," Gabi said gently.

"I did?" She glanced at Lion. "Didn't you ask about the windows?"

He nodded and won a smile from Gabi for his patience.

"Is that room empty?" Lion asked.

"Both of the rooms are," Maggie said. "The furniture was taken out some time ago. Quite honestly, the broken window was just the catalyst that got Gabi and me going on the redecoration. The painters are scheduled to start Monday; right, darling?"

"That's right. Lion, are you thinking someone might have gotten in through that broken window?"

His gaze rested thoughtfully on her. "Sometimes the simplest, most obvious explanation can be overlooked, because it *is* too simple, too obvious."

"I guess it could be possible," Maggie said slowly.

Bo frowned at her. "But *normally* you do keep the windows locked, don't you, Maggie?"

"Well, sure. It seems to make the guests feel better, so we try to be diligent about things like that."

"You *try*?" Lion asked. But if he'd found any fault with her casual attitude toward security, or with Bo for not thinking of the broken window sooner, he kept it to himself.

Gabi was once again grateful to him; however, she was extremely upset with herself. *She* should have thought of the window.

"If you don't mind, Maggie, I'd like to see those bedrooms." Lion glanced at Bo, making a point to include him. "I don't know if we'll find anything, but I also don't think it'd be a waste of time, do you, Bo?"

"No, I don't."

Maggie pushed away from the table and stood, and they all followed suit. "As soon as we find this odious person who's had the effrontery to break into my hotel and rob my guests, I'm going to personally knot the rope and hang him myself."

"You all go ahead," Gabi said. "I'll get the keys and meet you there."

"Are you sure?" Lion asked.

She nodded. "It'll be simpler this way, and it shouldn't take me long."

"We'll see you in a few minutes," he said with a smile that reached out and caressed her. Then he turned and followed the other two out of the restaurant.

Gabi stared after him, allowing herself the moment to savor the feeling of his smile. But in the next moment nausea swept over her and she had to grab for the support of the chair. How *stupid*, she thought, instantly realizing what had happened. She'd literally worried herself sick—over the thefts, over the identity of the thief, and most of all, over her love of Lion and his imminent departure. And the fact that everything might be concluded in the next half hour had brought her worries to a head.

She had to get control of her emotions, she told herself resolutely. The important thing was to find the two rings and Lion's watch. With stern determination she shook off the sick feeling and made her way out of the restaurant.

She encountered a large number of the reunion group milling in the lobby; even more of the group were outside on the porch and lawn. For people who had partied all night, they were amazingly happy and peppy, she reflected with admiration.

She ducked into the office, collected the keys, and very shortly was on her way to the back hallway, but a familiar voice stopped her in her tracks.

"*Gabi*, I've been looking everywhere for you. I've even left messages."

With a silent groan, she turned. "Good morning, Camilla. I'm sorry, I didn't get the messages, but would you mind if we talked later? I'm in sort of a hurry right now."

"I won't keep you long," Camilla said, practically bubbling with excitement. "But I *do* need to tell you the outcome of our séance last night."

"The séance?" She'd forgotten all about it.

"It was one of the most thrilling séances I've ever

conducted, lots and lots of energy zipping around. Gabi, I really *wish* you'd been there."

"Gee, yes, but listen—"

"Just one more second," Camilla said urgently. "My guides want me to tell you that you'll find the stolen things in a cozy, homey place."

"Excuse me?"

"They said and I quote: 'He took the things to a place that's very homey and very cozy.' "

"They said *he*?" she asked, intrigued in spite of herself.

"They said he." Camilla smiled. "That will help, won't it?"

The *name* of the thief would have been an even bigger help, she thought wryly. "I'm sure it will. Thank you, Camilla."

"I'm glad I could help. By the way, I won't be leaving until late this afternoon, so if you want me to try again—"

"No, no, that won't be necessary. I'll see you later."

Gabi hurried to where her grandmother, Bo, and Lion were waiting. "Sorry," she said breathlessly. "I was held up."

"No problem." Lion's voice was quiet, his hand soothing as he touched her shoulder.

Instantly she calmed. He really did have the most amazing effect on her, she thought. She inserted the key and opened the door to the first bedroom.

Navy drapes that had once hung at the windows

were neatly folded in a corner, Lion saw as he glanced around. Furrows in the carpet marked the size and former position of the furniture, and a blank piece of paper and two discarded coat hangers lay on the floor. "Is this the room you hit the ball into, Maggie?"

"No, it's the other one." She knelt to examine a particularly bad stain on the carpet. "Sometimes I wonder what the guests do in these rooms."

"Just sometimes?" Gabi asked dryly. "Ready to go next door, Lion?"

He nodded, taking in the lines of strain around her mouth and eyes. She was even more upset than she had been in the dining room, and he didn't like it. Solving the puzzle of the thefts for her sake had become more important to him than finding his watch.

The second bedroom was identical to the first in size and shape, but unlike the other, it was extremely messy. Lion studied the bits of duct tape, scraps of newspaper, and strips of toilet paper that littered the carpet, then walked over to the haphazard pile of badly frayed and torn green drapes.

"The window on the left is the one Gran knocked the ball through," Gabi murmured, then gestured to the large piece of cardboard propped against a wall. "We used that to cover the hole."

"How long did the cardboard stay up before the new window was in?"

"A couple of weeks," Maggie said.

Her flat tone made him look at her. Her usual high spirits had vanished, along with her color.

"The guys had to special-order the windows," she said, "then drive to Little Rock to pick them up."

Gabi bleakly shook her head. "It's painfully obvious that someone could have easily gotten in this way, even stayed hidden here for days at a time. All they had to do was stay away from the windows to keep from being seen."

Maggie rubbed her hand up and down her arm, as if she were suddenly cold. "You know, for some reason the thefts just haven't seemed real to me. But as soon as I walked in and saw the window, the reality hit me."

"Don't be too hard on yourself," Lion said. "You had no way of knowing."

"I own a hotel, Lion. It's my responsibility to know, to anticipate."

"I'm equally guilty, Gran. Maybe more so. But rehashing what we did and didn't do is useless. We need to go on the offensive now and look for anything that might help us. Bo, what about the possibility of fingerprints?"

"I'm sure going to give it a go." His distress had etched deep seams into his face. "The thing is, I'm afraid that most of the prints are going to belong to Bill and Mike."

Maggie rubbed her arm again. "I can't remember anything that's ever made me feel as vulnerable and as helpless as the idea that someone came and went at will from my home without my knowledge."

Bo reached out for her and drew her against him.

"This has been a shock to you, sweetheart. Come with me out to the car to get the fingerprinting kit. A little fresh air and sunshine will do you good."

She leaned against him. "Maybe you're right."

"He is," Gabi said. "By the time you two get back, we may have come up with something."

Maggie nodded. Keeping his arm around her, Bo guided her out of the room. But a few moments later she unexpectedly reappeared alone. "I told Bo I'd catch up to him," she said, crossing to Lion and taking his hand in hers. "I wanted to tell you how sorry I am, Lion."

"It's not necessary, Maggie. I know you are."

"It is necessary," she said earnestly. "You've been very kind and patient about all this, but I can imagine what you've been thinking. That's why I want you to believe me when I say Bo is simply wonderful at what he does, and I know he'll be successful with this."

He smiled gently down at her. "With you behind him, Maggie, how can he fail?"

"Thank you." Releasing his hand, she glanced at Gabi. "Stay here as long as you need, darling. I'll check on the guests."

"Okay, Gran."

He hadn't known how much he wanted to be alone with Gabi, he thought, until he finally was. "Maggie really does care about Bo, doesn't she?"

"Yes, she does." She clasped her hands. "Lion, I need to apologize to you too."

"As a matter of fact you don't."

Using even more gentleness than he had with

Maggie, he smiled at her. Now was the wrong time to tell her he loved her, but soon he was going to have to. He wouldn't be able to stop himself. He felt as if his love for her had filled him up and at any moment it would all come spilling out. "Look around and see if you notice anything that doesn't belong here."

"I've already done that and there's nothing." She bent to pick up some things off the carpet, then held out her hand so he could see. "An M&M with one M bitten off and a few peanut shells. Bob and Mike always bring snacks with them to keep up their energy." She brushed her hands free of the items.

"This thief is either the luckiest guy in the world or the smartest." He rubbed at his jaw.

"You're tired, aren't you?"

"We're *both* tired, Gabi."

"This is just so frustrating." With a soft, angry sound, she crossed to the window.

Her nerves were all on the surface, he thought, troubled.

"Let's try to think this through," she said, absently chewing on a thumbnail. "We know for sure that a diamond ring, a ruby ring, and an antique pocket watch have been stolen."

"That we're *aware* of," he said, speaking softly to mitigate the harshness of the truth. "Remember, someone could be missing something else and just hasn't realized it yet."

She threw a rueful grin over her shoulder at him. "Thanks for pointing that out."

He walked up behind her and eased his arms around her waist, and she settled back against him with a naturalness that made his heart skip a beat. "What else do we know for sure?"

"The thief obviously knows what's valuable and what's not, which would make him a professional, as Bo said . . . or simply a lover of beautiful things." She sighed.

He kissed the top of her silky head, inhaling the sweet light fragrance of her hair. "It's going to be okay."

"I'm sure you're right," she said, though her tone held no confidence. "You know, the *strangest* part of all is that the three thefts have happened on three different floors. That means the thief has had total access to the hotel, yet he's been able to move around without being detected."

"Sounds like a very discerning ghost to me."

"To me, too, unfortunately." She folded her arms over his at her waist and gave a light chuckle. "If a ghost really *has* been haunting the hotel all this time, and he's been either too contrary or too shy to let himself be known, Gran is going to be absolutely furious."

"All those missed opportunities for advertising, huh?"

"You got it."

She fell silent, and Lion was more than content to simply hold her and be with her. If he thought much harder about the thefts, he knew he would pick up the phone and call in help. But the last thing he wanted to do was further upset Gabi and Maggie, and he honestly hated to upstage Bo.

"I haven't seen Debra today," she murmured. "I hope she's all right."

"Do you have the same good wishes for Gordon?"

She softly laughed. "I guess so."

"What made you think about them?"

"My mind was wandering, and I was watching those two couples playing badminton and thinking about the reunion group. . . . Oh look, there's a rabbit at the edge of the woods." Suddenly she spun around and stared up at him in dismay.

"What?"

"I just realized that Debra's ring was stolen *after* the windows were replaced. When you and I went for our walk down to the creek, Bob and Mike were working here and would have known if anyone had been in the room. When I returned to the hotel around four, I didn't see them, so they'd already finished and gone. And Debra told us she went up to her room and took her ring off after five."

"Okay," he said, nodding, following her line of thinking. "So our guy entered another way, hid in another area. Gabi, as old as this hotel is, it must have all sorts of nooks and crannies and short, narrow passageways, not to mention the attics. For all we know, he could have walked in the front door."

She shook her head. "We always ask strangers who they're here to visit."

"Then, Gabi—the thief is someone you know."

He saw pain flash in her eyes before she turned

and leaned back against him. He wrapped his arms around her and gave her a quick hug. "You need to quit letting this get to you, Gabi."

"I know, but there's something very wrong about all this. It just doesn't make any sense."

"I can't argue with you there."

"The couples have gone. Guess they finished the game." Her soft, idle tone indicated her mind was wandering again. "Each year the leaves seem more gorgeous than the year before, but before we know it, they'll all have fallen and we'll be able to see through the trees."

"Do you still climb any of them?"

"Not in a long time." She chuckled. "But let me tell you, retreating to high ground sounds awfully good to me right now." All at once she uttered a loud gasp and broke away from him. *"Trees!"*

"Trees?" He turned her around, but even though she looked at him, he had the feeling she didn't see him. "Gabi?"

"Trees," she said slowly. "You said sometimes the simplest, most obvious answer is overlooked . . . and Camilla told me—" She bolted for the door. *"Come on."*

"Wait." He barely managed to grab her arm and stop her. "Where are we going?"

"I've got to check something out," she said with breathless impatience. "Stay or go."

He immediately released her. "If you're going, I'm going."

She hurried out of the room, picked up speed as she jogged down the hall, then burst outside. Lion saw her glance back once to check that he was behind her and then she took off across the lawn, running as fast as she could.

If she'd looked back again, he thought, she would have seen him grinning like a fool. He found it hilariously funny that this time he wasn't just *following* her, he was actually *chasing* her.

She stopped at the edge of the woods and waited for him. "Is this it?" he asked when he reached her.

"No, but we're going to have to go slower now. Come on."

"Where have I heard that before?" he murmured, but Gabi didn't hear him, because despite what she'd said, she was already ahead of him, setting a predictably fast pace along the path they'd taken yesterday. This time he stayed even with her, and she didn't stop again until they reached the creek.

"You see that hollowed-out tree stump over there?" She pointed toward a large stump. "The one that looks about four or five feet high and is maybe twenty feet up from the creek."

"What about it?"

"The raccoons around here usually make their nests up in the trees, but this past summer I've seen Rocky going in and out of that stump more than once."

"And you're thinking *what* exactly?" he asked.

"I'm thinking that Rocky could be our thief."

Rocky. It made perfect sense, he thought.

"Come on. We're going to have to be careful."

Gabi moved off briskly, expertly picking her way over the rough, uneven ground, and around rocks and prickly outgrowths. Lion was close behind her. A few yards away from the stump, they both slowed and eased their way up to it.

Lion knelt and bent his head to look in. "Rocky's not home," he said, and gazed in wonder at the jumble in the raccoon's nest.

Gabi knelt beside him and peeked in. "How on *earth* did he manage to get all that?"

"We'll have to ask him," he said, grinning as he recognized the strips of green drapery. There were also rags, whole sections of newspaper, bits of toilet paper, and . . .

"The *rings*." Gabi sighed with relief.

He reached into the stump and brought out a handful of things. "And my watch."

"Thank *heavens*."

"And two cuff links that don't match."

Gabi took a second look into the stump. "My new blue *blouse* is in there."

Lion brought out another handful. "Recognize any of this?"

"I'm afraid so." She pointed. "That bracelet is Gran's and there's part of an old slip of mine that I thought I'd thrown away, and that earring looks familiar. I'll have to show some of this to the staff."

"I'll say this for the little guy," he drawled. "He's got an eye for decorating."

Gabi gazed at him, then threw back her head and laughed.

It was an incredibly beautiful sound, filled with relief and happiness, Lion thought. He listened as it pealed through the woods and *felt* it as it pierced straight into his heart.

ELEVEN

The late-afternoon shadows crawled their way across the front lawn as Lion rocked on the porch and waited until he could be alone with Gabi. A few feet away from him at the top of the steps, she was seeing the last of the reunion group on their way. She still looked tired, he reflected, but at least she was no longer worried about the thefts. And after everyone was gone, they could rest together.

"I can't thank you enough for finding my ring," he heard Debra King say to Gabi.

"Believe me," she said, "I'm as relieved as you."

Debra threw a quick glance over her shoulder. "Before Gordon gets here, I wanted you to know that we stayed in our room today and were finally able to talk everything out and work through our problems."

"You don't owe me an explanation, Debra."

"Strictly speaking, no. But after the trouble last night, I thought you deserved one, a very *short* one.

You see, in high school, I went steady with Douglas, who was Mr. All-Everything, and I never paid much notice to Gordon until, *luckily*, we went off to the same college. I was able to really get to know him there, and I fell deeply in love with him, and we've had a wonderful marriage." She paused. "But the reunion brought out insecurities in my husband I never knew he had."

"I'm not sure I knew either," Gordon said as he joined the two women.

"You heard?" Debra asked.

"Just the last part." He slid his arm around her waist. "I know I acted like a complete jerk this weekend, Gabi, but the thought of Debra seeing Douglas again made me a little crazy. I was so afraid she'd decide she'd made a mistake all those years ago when she chose me over Douglas."

Debra smiled at him, then looked at Gabi. "I never loved Douglas. I married *Gordon* because it was *him* I loved."

Gordon turned a bright pink. "I feel pretty stupid. And, Gabi, I sincerely apologize for every asinine thing I did or said. If it helps, I paid for it with a hangover that made my head feel like it was coming apart."

"I'm sorry," Gabi said, then ruined her sympathetic words by laughing. "At any rate, all's well that ends well. You two come back and see us."

"We will," Debra said. "In fact, brace yourself. We've all been talking about returning for our thirtieth reunion."

"That would be *great*," Gabi said sincerely.

Gordon went over to shake Lion's hand. "Thank you for seeing that I got coffee last night."

"No problem. Have a safe journey home."

"We will." They descended the steps and disappeared around the side of the hotel to the parking lot.

"How are you holding up, Gabi?"

"Fine, but it will definitely be an early night for me."

"For me too."

"Gabi, I just *heard*." Camilla rushed out onto the porch, her long hair tied back with a scarf, a weekend bag in her hand. "It was a *raccoon*."

Gabi grinned. "An extremely smart, curious, dexterous raccoon."

"I never knew before that raccoons liked shiny objects."

"Well, obviously Rocky does. In fact, after digging around in that tree stump, I can tell you there isn't much he *doesn't* like. And by the way, your guides were right. We found the stolen things in his nest, which was *very* cozy and homey."

"I'm glad. I'm also glad the disturbance that's been hovering around you all weekend is gone. But now I see a sadness."

"I know," Gabi said softly. "But it'll pass."

Lion stopped rocking. He'd thought Gabi was simply tired, but now he realized Camilla was right. There were subtle signs of sadness in Gabi's expression. Why? he wondered. And what could he do to fix it?

"I've got to be going," Camilla said, "but please don't hesitate to call me if you need me. My phone number is on my bill. Oh, and I *will* be back." She practically skipped down the stairs to the drive. "This hotel has the most *fabulous* vibes of any place I've ever been."

"We'll look forward to seeing you again." Gabi waved good-bye, then moved over to the rocking chair next to Lion and dropped into it. "Did you get that? *Fabulous* vibes."

"I have to agree with her."

"I think Camilla was the last of her group. At least I hope she was."

"Why are you sad?" he asked quietly.

"Sad? Oh, you must have heard Camilla." She rested her head against the rocking chair's high back. "I'm not sad, just tired."

"You're also sad. Why?"

She fixed her gaze on a point near the horizon and remained silent so long, he began to wonder if she was going to answer him.

"Did you hear the reunion group saying good-bye to each other?" she asked after a time, as if it was a subject they'd been talking about.

"Some of them."

"Everyone promised to stay in touch, and I'm sure they all have the best of intentions. They may even make the effort a couple of times, but then they'll get busy and time will pass—" She broke off as her grandmother strolled out the door. "Has everyone left who was scheduled to, Gran?"

Maggie nodded. "Including one who wasn't scheduled. *Lawrence.* Since he's no longer a suspect, he decided to continue his tour of America. I suggested the Southwest area as his next stop. I think he'll enjoy it."

Lion grinned. "Got rid of him, huh?"

"Sure did."

"What about the Wentworths?" With a push of her foot, Gabi sent her chair slowly rocking.

"They're staying another week." Maggie leaned against one of the posts and looked at Lion. "So what do you think, handsome? I bet you never knew a quiet, out-of-the-way place like the St. Armand could be so exciting."

"It's been an eventful weekend, all right," he said, resigned to the fact that he was going to have to wait a little longer to find out what was bothering Gabi.

"Personally," she said with wry humor, "I've had all the *eventfulness* I can take for a while."

"I'd like that in writing, please." Gabi's tone held blatant disbelief.

Lion nodded toward the car that was just pulling up. "Now we'll see if she's serious or not. Bo's here."

Maggie straightened away from the post and avidly watched as the sheriff climbed out of his car. "Why, Bo, what a *nice* surprise."

"Surprise? I told you I'd be back."

"Really? I must have forgotten."

"Here we go again," Gabi murmured, making Lion chuckle.

Bo propped a booted foot on the lower step. "I

was wondering, Maggie, if you'd like to come over to my place tonight."

"Well, now, I don't know," she drawled. "What did you have in mind?"

He shrugged. "A couple of steaks on the grill, maybe a bottle of wine and some nice music on the stereo."

Gabi shot out of the rocking chair and grabbed hold of her grandmother's arm. "She accepts, Bo."

Maggie pressed her hand over her heart. "Oh, no—I mean, I'm not at all sure . . ."

"Oh, for heaven sakes, Gran, let him win. *Go.*" With a shove, she sent Maggie staggering down the steps—right into Bo's arms.

The last part had been strictly Maggie's doing, and not the result of Gabi's shove, Lion noted, highly amused. "Have a great time, you two."

"And don't feel you have to come home early," Gabi said.

With a big, wide grin, Bo ushered Maggie into his car. "See you all later."

"Make that *much* later, okay?" Gabi called out.

"I'll do my best to oblige." Still grinning, he ducked into the car and drove away.

"Guess what?" Lion asked, pushing out of the rocking chair. "As hard as it is to believe, I think we're actually alone."

"Not really. The Wentworths are still here, along with a skeleton staff."

"I'll kill anyone who interrupts us, I don't care *who* they are." He smiled at her. "So finish telling me why the idea that the reunion group might not keep in touch with each other makes you so sad."

"It doesn't. I was just making a general comment." She glanced at him, then away. "I hope you don't mind, but I'm going to retire early tonight."

"I don't mind at all as long as I'm with you."

"You won't be," she said, making a quick, unexpected move toward the door.

She was halfway across the lobby when, as he'd done so often this past weekend, he caught her and pulled her to a halt. "What's going on with you, Gabi?"

She sighed. "When are you leaving, Lion?"

"*That's* what's bothering you?" His brow furrowed. "That I'll be leaving."

"Why does that surprise you?" Her short laugh sounded brittle. "From the very first moment I saw you, I accepted that you wouldn't be here long and that as soon as possible you'd be going back to your own life. But just because I accepted it doesn't mean I can say good-bye to you without being a trifle upset."

"A trifle? Gabi, when I leave here, there'll be no reason to be upset, a trifle or otherwise. I want you to come with me. I—"

She held up her hand. "*Don't.*"

"Don't what? Ask you to come with me? Why not? I *care* about you, and I know you care about me. You're not the kind of woman who would have slept with me otherwise, and whether you believe it or not, where you're concerned, I'm not that type of man."

A hint of moisture glinted in her eyes. "You care about me?"

"Yes, very much. I'm sorry, I should have said it much sooner, but—"

"This is all impossible." She touched her forehead. "I can't think."

"You need sleep, but try to hang on a little longer." He took her hand and pulled her toward the elevator. "Please note that this time *I'm* the one who is leading and *you're* the one who is following. It's a nice change, don't you think?"

"Lion, stop. I'm not going anywhere with you."

She was looking at him as if he had two heads, and he didn't blame her a bit. At the elevator, he punched the up button and the doors swished open. "Come on." He gently tugged at her hand until he had her inside, then pressed the sixth-floor button.

Wearily, she leaned against the back wall. "What are you doing, Lion?"

In his lifetime, he'd experienced great pain and great joy, but never the anxiety he was experiencing at this moment. "In spite of the weekend having been crazy and chaotic, you and I managed to have a wonderful time and get to know each other. Now the chaos is over, and you and I are still here together, and I—"

"I'm still here because I *live* here." The elevator stopped and the doors opened, but she didn't move.

"Will you please come with me to my suite so that we can talk?"

"First," she said evenly, "there's something you

should know. Gold Springs may be a small, quaint town, but its citizens are not at all backward and neither am I."

He punched the hold button. "I never suggested you were."

"The point is this, Lion. I'll never regret making love with you. I made the decision with my eyes open and with no expectations of anything more from you than that time together. I never *once* thought I'd be going with you when you left, and what's more, I *won't*."

Acid churned in his stomach. "Why?"

She shrugged. "Let's just say I'd make a really bad girlfriend."

He studied her, absorbing how pale she looked and how close to being emotionally spent she appeared. "There are a great many things wrong with what you're thinking, Gabi, and it's entirely my fault." He held out his hand to her. "Please?"

With obvious reluctance, she took it. "Let's make this fast."

"I'll do my best," he said.

Inside the suite, Gabi collapsed into one of the big easy chairs, but when she looked at him, her expression was full of strength. "Okay, I'm here."

He smiled. "You're not going to make this easy on me, are you?"

"Maybe if I knew what was on your mind, I could offer some help."

He couldn't help but chuckle. "I think I'll decline that particular offer for now. You helped me on Friday and I've had trouble knowing which way was up ever since."

Her reply was unexpectedly soft and serious. "Friday seems a long time ago."

"That's because so much has happened."

"True."

Touching her, even if only to hold her hand, would have made him feel so much better. But the big overstuffed chair was almost an island unto itself; when she'd chosen it, she'd physically isolated herself.

He moved in front of her. "Gabi?"

She looked up at him. "Yes?"

"When I said I wanted you to come with me, I wasn't asking you to live with me or to merely become my girlfriend."

"What did you have in mind? A sort of extended date?"

"No." Silently cursing at himself, he thrust his fingers through his hair. The words he wanted to say were all tangled up together and weren't coming out right.

She crossed her arms beneath her breasts and regarded him with mock thoughtfulness. "I just realized I should ask where you're going. It could be a place I've always wanted to visit."

With an abruptness that was deliberate, he dropped to one knee and clasped her hand before she could react. "Okay, I'm going to try this again. When I told you I wanted you to leave with me, it was a knee-jerk, badly stated response, because I wanted to keep you with me."

"I see," she said in a tone that told him she was finally attempting to understand. "So you're saying you wanted the good times to continue awhile longer?"

"No, I'm not." He grimaced in self-disgust. "You're tired, I'm tired. I'm trying very hard not to frighten you away, and in the process, I'm saying this all wrong."

"I'm not afraid of you, Lion. I never have been."

"No, you haven't, but that's not what I meant." He paused, thinking. "All right, as straightforwardly as I know how, I'm going to try to tell you how I feel about you."

Confusion and dread flickered across her face. "No—"

"Stop," he said softly. "Wait. It's all really so simple. I *love* you, Gabi. I love you so much, I hurt from it. I love you more than I ever thought it possible for a man to love a woman."

Her eyes slowly widened in disbelief.

"Don't do that. I know we haven't known each other long. I know I should probably *court* you, but the truth is I'm not traditional and I never will be." Surging to his feet, he pulled her with him, then gazed deeply into her eyes. "And here's more truth for you. Now that I've found you, I don't want to be without you, not even for a minute. I want to marry you as soon as possible. I want you to stay with me forever. And I *never*, ever want to let you out of my sight." He drew in a shaky breath, exhaled it, and studied her closely. A calm had settled over her and he had no idea what she was thinking. "Well?"

"Are you through telling me what it is you want?"

"There's just one more thing." He crushed his mouth down on hers and kissed her until she was weak against him and her hands were clinging to him. Gradually, cautiously, he lifted his head. This moment was so important, yet he'd never felt so uncertain. "Just answer yes or no. Do you love me?"

"Yes."

He'd so desperately wanted her to say yes, he wasn't sure he could trust what he heard. "Will you marry me?"

"Yes."

He still couldn't let himself believe it.

"Now can I say something else?" she asked.

"Only if it's something I'm going to like."

She slowly smiled. "Take me to bed and make love with me."

"You're very, very lucky," he said with a gruff huskiness, and swung her into his arms. "I happen to like your request."

She began to laugh, and the clear, glistening sound of her happiness swirled around him and into him. And he began to laugh with her, knowing with absolute certainty that they would spend the rest of their lives laughing together, loving together, and enjoying every single moment. Together.

THE EDITORS' CORNER

What better way to celebrate the holidays than with four sensual and exciting new LOVESWEPTs. Whether they're searching for treasure or battling bad guys, our heroes are sure to deliver thrills, laughs, and passion as they do whatever they must to win the hearts of our heroines. So curl up in your favorite chair with a blanket and a cup of hot cocoa and enjoy!

Starting off our fabulous lineup is Marcia Evanick with **TANGLED UP IN BLUE**, LOVESWEPT #818. He's expecting a gray-haired housesitter who plays bingo when she isn't baking cookies or dusting, but when Matt Stone returns unannounced, he discovers instead a golden-haired nymph splashing naked in his pool! Beulah Crawford, nicknamed Blue, is the picture of sweet chaos, a delightful scamp who revels in living for the moment. Now all Matt has to do is make her believe that family isn't just an impossible dream. Hailed by *Romantic Times* for "delighting readers with her marvelous blend of love and laughter," Marcia Evanick won't let readers down in this funny tale of cat and mouse romance.

Watch out, villains! Cynthia Powell has found a **HERO FOR HIRE**, LOVESWEPT #819. Cade Jackson has a face too hard to be handsome, Martinique Duval decides, and a smile just lethal enough to make a good girl want to be bad! Tracking his quarry has led the tough bounty hunter straight to this wildfire angel, but keeping her safe means risking a heart he didn't know he had. Can her innocence give a reluctant hero with a scarred soul a reason to stop running forever? Rising star Cynthia Powell proves once again that every man is susceptible to the call of true love.

Talented newcomer Eve Gaddy believes that two people in love can never be **TOO CLOSE FOR COMFORT**, LOVESWEPT #820. Jack Corelli vows to keep Marissa Fairfax alive to testify, but guarding the cool trauma surgeon means long, hot hours in close quarters with a woman who challenges him to break all of his rules! She barely trembles when held at gunpoint, but Jack's slow, sizzling attack on her mouth makes her shiver and burn. Together, this wounded hero and the lady he'd die to protect must learn to silence ghosts and survive a desperate betrayal. Eve Gaddy takes readers on a heart-palpitating ride as she weaves a tale you won't soon forget!

When you're gambling with love, everything is **UP FOR GRABS**, LOVESWEPT #821, by Kristen Robinette. Jesse McCain steps onto her land without asking, a bold buccaneer who knows the stormy-eyed lady won't deny him a chance to dig up her property—and her past! Targeted by a grin full of promises, Lauren Adams feels her resistance melt, but the brash archeologist isn't telling her all he knows. Still, she isn't one to back down from a challenge, so she follows Jesse down an unknown path and ends up losing her heart to a road warrior with a secret. In a debut that readers are sure to enjoy, Kristen delivers a top-notch romance full of tenderness and passion.

Happy reading!

With warmest wishes,

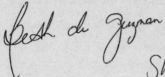

Beth de Guzman
Senior Editor

Shauna Summers
Editor

P.S. Watch for these Bantam women's fiction titles coming in January: From Sandra Brown, the author of twenty-nine *New York Times* bestselling titles, comes **HAWK O'TOOLE'S HOSTAGE**, a riveting contemporary romance in which a woman is held hostage by a desperate man . . . and a desperate desire. Now available in paperback, **THE UGLY DUCKLING** is a thrilling novel of contemporary suspense by *New York Times* bestselling author Iris Johansen. From Susan Johnson, mistress of erotic romance, comes **WICKED,** a spectacular romance of suspense and seduction. And finally, **HEART OF THE FALCON** by Suzanne Robinson captures the passion of Egypt as a defiant beauty fights to regain her birthright. Don't miss the previews of these exceptional novels in next month's LOVESWEPTs. And immediately following this page, sneak a peek at the Bantam women's fiction titles on sale *now*!

For current information on Bantam's women's fiction, visit our new web site, *Isn't It Romantic*, at the following address: **http://www.bdd.com/romance**

Don't miss these extraordinary books
by your favorite Bantam authors

On sale in November:

AFTER CAROLINE
by Kay Hooper

BREAKFAST IN BED
by Sandra Brown

DON'T TALK TO STRANGERS
by Bethany Campbell

LORD SAVAGE
by Patricia Coughlin

LOVE'S A STAGE
by Sharon and Tom Curtis

from

Kay Hooper

Her sensuous and evocative voice has made her a
nationally bestselling author, and now she weaves a
haunting new tale of contemporary suspense, a
gripping emotional tapestry of two women bound
together in the desperation of one fatal moment—
and the urgent need to uncover the truth.

AFTER CAROLINE

Joanna Flynn was lucky to be alive. Twice in a matter
of minutes she almost died on a patch of oil-slicked
highway. But when the doctors told her that she
would suffer no lasting effects, they were wrong. For
that night the dreams began. . . .

They were of a house perched high above the sea,
of a ticking clock, and the lingering scent of roses. Yet
night after night Joanna awoke with a sense of panic.
Terror lingered throughout her days, urging her to do
something—but what? Then two strangers on the
street called her Caroline, and Joanna knew she had
to find an explanation for what was happening, or
she'd lose her mind.

What she finally uncovered was an obituary for a
woman named Caroline McKenna—a woman who
looked enough like her to be her twin, a woman who
was killed in a car accident on the same day Joanna
should have perished. Now her torturous nightmares
and a tenuous connection have brought Joanna three
thousand miles across country to the town where
Caroline lived—and died. Almost everyone has stories

to tell about Cliffside's leading lady, and yet no one seems to have known her. Was she the shy wife or the seductress of men? The devoted mother or the selfish beauty?

Too soon Joanna realizes that it's not her sanity at stake, but her life. For unraveling the mystery of Caroline means uncovering the secrets in this picturesque town, secrets someone may have killed to hide. And that someone appears all too willing to kill again.

AVAILABLE IN HARDCOVER

Sandra Brown

Her novels are sensual and moving, compelling and richly satisfying. Now the *New York Times* bestselling author of *Heaven's Price* captures the wrenching dilemma of a woman tempted by an unexpected—and forbidden—love. . . .

BREAKFAST IN BED

Hurt one too many times in the past, Sloan Fairchild is convinced that she will never be able to trust her heart to a man again. Instead, she pours all her energy into making a success of her elegant San Francisco bed-and-breakfast inn. But when her best friend asks her to house her fiancé for a month, Sloan opens the doors of Fairchild House to Carter Madison . . . and meets a man who turns her world—and her concept of herself—upside down.

Carter, a bestselling author, is looking for a little peace and quiet so he can finish his latest novel before his wedding. The last thing he expects is to find himself instantly attracted to his hostess—or her to him. As the days pass, Sloan tries to ignore the feelings this handsome, disturbingly perceptive man stirs in her . . . tries to stop herself from dreaming dreams that can never be. But as Carter reveals his overwhelming desire for her, Sloan is left to struggle against her own deepest longing: to know just once how it feels to be truly cherished.

Caught between love and loyalty to her best friend, Sloan must search her soul and make a choice: to love for the moment, walk away forever, or fight to have it all.

AVAILABLE IN PAPERBACK

A seductive game of hide-and-seek

Bethany Campbell

Nationally bestselling author of *See How They Run*

DON'T TALK TO STRANGERS

One by one the women were disappearing. Each had been young, vulnerable . . . and spending time "chatting" on the Internet with a mysterious stranger. It was Carrie Blue's job to track down that stranger, to put herself on the Internet in the guise of a lonely young student and smoke out a cunningly seductive killer. But soon she is drawn inexorably into a world where truth is indistinguishable from fiction . . . and it proves far more difficult than she could have imagined to resist the lure of a twisted mind—one that may already have figured out who Carrie is, and marked her as his next kill. . . .

"Carrie, look at me."

She struggled to keep control of her voice. "No."

"Yes," he said. "Are you afraid to? Why?"

She let her hands drop to her lap, straightened, and gave him a resentful glance. But she couldn't hold his gaze, and looked at the window instead, where the rain blurred the glass to a gray translucence.

"I know you were in the pub last night, alone," he said. "Then the Highwayman came in. You broke your connection, and he logged off immediately after. He never came back."

"How do you know all this?"

"I've learned a few tricks. I can see you from a

distance. Where you are and who you're with. But not what you're doing."

"You learned to do that from reading the archives?"

"Yes."

"You spy on me?"

"I monitor you and Brooke. Every fifteen minutes."

Carrie shrugged and said nothing.

"So what happened with the Highwayman?" he asked again.

"That's my business."

"It's my business too. There's a girl in a morgue in Illinois. Doesn't that matter?"

Her cheeks went hot and she shot him a glance of rebuke. "Of course it matters."

"So what about this Highwayman? What in God's name went on between you?"

Oh, hell, she thought wearily. If Hayden wanted the truth so much, she'd give it to him, right between the eyes. She no longer gave a damn about her pride, and it was Hayden who'd led her into this nasty farce.

"He was drunk. He wanted netsex. I said I wouldn't, not with someone who wouldn't tell me his name. So I broke the connection."

"I tried your private line," Hayden said. "It was busy. He phoned you?"

Carrie took a deep breath and told him what Paul Johnson had said. "I believe him. It makes me feel sick. This poor, disabled kid in love with a girl who doesn't exist. I want to hang myself."

Her chin trembled, and she thought, *I will not cry again. I will not let him see me cry. No one has seen me cry for ten years.*

Hayden's expression grew guarded. He might have been surprised or repelled, but all he said was "Carrie, Monica Toussant and Gretchen Small believed somebody too. What if it's not true? It's a damn good story. He loves you, and only you can heal him."

Carrie resisted the desire to pick up the coffee mug and fling it at his head. "If he's lying, he's contemptible. If he isn't, I'm contemptible. And if he's telling the truth, I couldn't stand it. The very thought makes me feel slimy."

He frowned. "He says his name's Paul Johnson? And he's not a citizen of the U.S.? How many guys do you suppose are named Paul Johnson in North America? He's got your phone number, but do you have his?"

"No," Carrie said. "So what?"

"He's living with a married sister, but you don't know her last name?"

She tilted her chin to a rebellious angle. "No."

"So how do you trace him, Carrie? How do you know he's for real? Do you have his address?"

"No," she said. "Stop trying to change my mind."

"I've got to. What if he's not some poor, disabled kid who thinks he's in love with you? What if he's an excellent liar who's stalking you?"

"What if he's not?" she challenged. "What if he's a twenty-three-year-old man who may never walk again? What then?"

"If we find out that's true, you let him down easy. It's not as if the two of you really know each other."

"He wants to have netsex with me, for God's sake. And I've encouraged him. I've let him hold me in his arms, hug me, kiss me."

He searched her face for a moment. Her confused emotions grew more tumultuous. *Something's going to happen*, she thought. *And I haven't got the strength to stop it.*

He said, "He's never touched you."

He put his hand to her face, his fingertips grazing first her cheekbone, then her jawline. With thumb and forefinger he lightly cupped her chin. "This is touching."

Her heart thudded crazily. She told herself, *Don't let this happen.*

"And he hasn't really kissed you," he breathed.

He tipped her face to his and brought his mouth to bear on hers, gently at first, then more hungrily.

Oh, God, oh, God, oh, God, she thought, her heart leaping.

He's real. He's real.

She had eight weeks to tame a savage—
and to fall in love.

LORD SAVAGE
by
Patricia Coughlin

The request was impossible. Unthinkable. And unavoidable. Ariel Halliday couldn't refuse the head of the Penrose School when he asked her to take on the particularly difficult assignment—not if she wanted to stay in his good graces. Now she has only eight weeks to transform a savage raised on a distant Pacific island into a gentleman. Yet nothing could prepare her for the darkly handsome "pupil" who is the heir apparent of the Marquis of Sage.

Ariel stepped inside the room and heard the door shut behind her with a click that sounded as irrevocable as a gunshot. She closed her eyes briefly, caught her breath, and took a determined step forward.

"Good afternoon," she said. Another breath. In. Out. She could do this. "I'm Miss Halliday. Miss Ariel Halliday. I know that you're Leon Nicholas Duvanne, the fifth Marquis of Sage. I'm just not sure that you know it yet," she added ruefully.

She set the tray on the small table a few feet from his cot.

"Of course you have a whole mouthful of other titles I shall not even attempt to recite for you now. I believe Lord Sav—Sage will suit nicely for the time being."

Ninny, she thought. Such a slip of the tongue might have made for a most uneasy moment. That is, if he even understood a word she was saying. There was still no indication he did. For that matter, there was no obvious sign the man was alive, but for the slow, steady rise and fall of his very imposing chest.

Ariel, trying not to stare in fascination at the wedge of silky dark chest hair, wet her suddenly dry lips with her tongue.

"Proper manners," she began, "dictate that a gentleman rise when a lady enters the room and greet her by title and name. I am prepared to overlook your failure to do so on this occasion, overtaxed as I'm sure you must be from your obviously high level of exertion thus far today." He offered no response to her sarcasm.

"I do believe, however," she continued, "that in consideration of the fact that I have gone to considerable trouble to bring you tea, you could at the very least turn your head and acknowledge that I am speaking to you."

To her amazement, the dark head began to slowly turn her way. He understood, she thought excitedly. Either her words or her chilly tone, she couldn't be certain which, but he had clearly understood something. And he had responded.

Her excitement turned to apprehension as he proceeded to swing his feet to the floor and stand, facing her fully. She fought an urge to step back. He made no move to come closer, however, and her heartbeat gradually slowed to as near normal as she expected it to be while she remained confined there alone with him.

His gaze caught and held hers and Ariel found that the effect of his silent presence was even more daunting when he was staring directly into her eyes. He was, she concluded, without question the most beautiful man she had ever seen. Never before had she thought to describe a man as beautiful, but the word came to her easily and naturally when she gazed at Lord Sage's serene face and strong, lean body. He appeared to her as masculine perfection, chiseled by the hand of the greatest master of all.

His cheekbones were aristocratically high, his jaw

beneath the short black beard classically square, his mouth full, with just enough of a slant to add interest to his otherwise perfect face. A stray lock of his long, raven hair hung loosely across his forehead, and his eyes, deep-set and almond-shaped, were a quite extraordinary shade. Brown velvet swirled with gold, dark and bright at once, like sunlight on ancient brass. Tiger's eyes, Ariel mused, thinking of the gemstone by that name. Hard and gleaming and exotic.

At that moment the expression in his remarkable eyes was nether warm nor cold, neither friendly nor antagonistic. It was shuttered. She felt certain that the man was no dolt, and that although he would not permit her to be privy to it, there was a great deal of thought and evaluation going on inside his head. In fact, some instinct warned her that his lordship was taking her measure just as calculatedly as she was taking his.

She straightened, smoothing a few stray wisps of light brown hair. Why hadn't she taken more pains in arranging the chignon at the back of her neck that morning? she lamented. And perhaps worn a newer dress? One in a more flattering color? She quickly marshaled her thoughts, reminding herself that she did not possess a newer dress and that gray was a most serviceable hue for everyday wear and besides that, it mattered not at all what the man before her thought of her appearance.

Without warning he shook back his hair, dislodging the lock that hung over his forehead to reveal a two-inch-long scar there. The imperfection, which would have marred the appeal of most men, enhanced his instead. For the first time Ariel noticed the array of other small marks and scars that covered his body, souvenirs, it seemed to her, of a life far more reckless and exciting than her own. Feeling a mixture of curiosity and envy, she lifted her gaze to his to find him watching her with his eyes narrowed in suspicion.

The eagerly awaited reissue of a memorable classic
by

Sharon and Tom Curtis

LOVE'S A STAGE

Frances Atherton came to London to explore the plot that sent her father to prison. But she never imagined that she, too, would be held captive—by the charms of London's most scandalous playwright and fascinating rake. Devastatingly handsome Lord David Landry has charmed any number of women, and makes it clear that Frances is next. . . .

He had said there were two reasons he had been following her on Charles Street, the first being that he was concerned about her safely reaching her destination. It was true, Frances thought, that she might have had a difficult time locating her great-aunt's new address without him.

"But what was the second?"

"I beg your pardon?" he said, sending his sweet smiling glance at her.

"The second reason you followed me."

He looked, if not precisely surprised, then a little curious; he studied her face as if to revise a prior impression. His eyes were bright and kind as he said, "Miss Atherton, surely you must know."

The wind's mischievous fingers had loosened her bonnet strings. She retied them rapidly as she walked.

"Well, I don't. And as we've been walking along, it occurs to me to wonder why you would want to spend your time helping strangers around the streets, because I can see now, even if I did not at first, that you are quite a brilliant man."

It was his turn to be amused. "*Thank* you, Miss Atherton. You honor me too much. Do you know, though, that if you continue in that vein, I will find myself revising my previous estimate on the size of your hamlet downward. Hasn't anyone ever tried to seduce you?"

Seduce. She knew the word, of course, but it had previously played so minute a part in her vocabulary that she was forced to think a moment to recall its meaning. She gasped when she remembered and said simply, "No."

"That's quite an oversight on somebody's part." A crowded street corner was not the setting a man of his vast experience would have chosen to make a declaration of desire, nor was a bald statement of fact as likely to produce a successful result as were patience and attentive intimacy. To have ignored her direct appeal for an explanation, though, would have amounted to a deception alien to his nature.

A grin touched his lips as he noted they had arrived almost at the ornamental porch that marked the entrance to Miss Isles's apartments—at least, when she demanded the return of her case, she would have only a short space to carry it. "Miss Atherton," he said gently, "I would like to be more than friends with you."

Frances's young life had been devoted to duty and service. She was assistant mother to eight younger siblings, confidante and soul mate to her papa and aide-de-camp to her unworldly, domestically inclined mama. Excepting her brothers, the only young men Frances knew were the fishermen's sons from her village, any one of whom would have been too shy to woo the parson's lovely, intelligent daughter. There had been no proposals, proper or improper, in Miss Atherton's life, and while she might daydream in modesty of the former, it had never crossed her mind that she might ever be in a position to receive the latter. So unexpected was the declaration that Miss Atherton was not completely sure of his intention until he said helpfully, "Yes, Miss Atherton, I meant precisely what you think I meant."

To say that Frances was shocked would have been greatly to understate the case; in fact, she was astonished. She had never been encouraged to think of herself as pretty. As a result, she did not, and it came as a surprise to her that she could somehow have inspired those sentiments in any gentleman, particularly one who, it was quite obvious, could hardly have suffered from a lack of feminine companionship. Her incredulous surprise, however, was soon trampled by a flaming wrath.

"I suppose you think," she said dangerously, "that because I *allowed* you to talk to me on the street you can insult me!"

Capped in her shabby brown bonnet and cloaked in her puritanical morality, she had for him the quaint charm of a delightfully apt cliché. They had reached Miss Isles's building, so he set her case on the low porch before the door and took Miss Atherton's flushed cheeks leisurely between his palms, forcing her to look into his sparkling green eyes.

"Never, Prudence," he said with what Frances regarded as an odious tranquillity, "is it an insult to tell a woman that you find her so attractive that you would like to—"

Miss Atherton stopped his words by clapping her mittened hands over her ears in a gesture rendered unfortunately inefficient by the oversized contours of her bonnet. She removed her face from his hold with so forceful a back-step that if it were not for his steadying hands on her shoulders, she would surely have fallen.

"It is always, *al-ways*," she said furiously, "an insult unless preceded by a marriage vow."

Releasing her shoulders, he walked to the heavy

oak door and held it open for her. Miss Atherton marched past and found they had entered a narrow hall lined with marble wallpaper in yellow and brown. An interior door lay to the right of the entrance, and a wooden open-newel stair lit by a single lamp led to an upper landing. He lifted her case inside the threshold and shut the outer door behind them.

There was both rueful self-knowledge and compassion in his smile as he said, "That's one game I don't play, Prudence. I doubt if I'll ever be able to make that type of commitment to a woman. Honestly, sweetheart, there's very little chance I'd marry you."

Miss Atherton came to a full rolling boil. "Well, there is *no* chance that I would marry you!" She stormed to the door like a tidal wave and pounded against it with her fist.

On sale in December:

HAWK O'TOOLE'S HOSTAGE
by Sandra Brown

THE UGLY DUCKLING
by Iris Johansen

WICKED
by Susan Johnson

HEART OF THE FALCON
by Suzanne Robinson

DON'T MISS THESE FABULOUS
BANTAM WOMEN'S FICTION TITLES

On Sale in November

AFTER CAROLINE by Kay Hooper

"Kay Hooper is a master storyteller." —Tami Hoag

The doctors told Joanna Flynn that she shouldn't suffer any ill effects from her near-fatal accidents, but then the dreams began. Now she must find an explanation, or she'll lose her mind—perhaps even her life.

___09948-5 $21.95/$26.95

BREAKFAST IN BED

by sizzling New York Times bestseller Sandra Brown

Sandra Brown captures the wrenching dilemma of a woman tempted by an unexpected—and forbidden—love in this classic novel, now available in paperback.

___57158-3 $5.50/$7.50

DON'T TALK TO STRANGERS

by national bestseller Bethany Campbell

"A master storyteller of stunning intensity." —Romantic Times

Young women are disappearing after meeting a mysterious stranger on the Internet, and it's Carrie Blue's job to lure the killer . . . without falling prey to his cunningly seductive mind.

___56973-2 $5.50/$7.50

LORD SAVAGE by the acclaimed Patricia Coughlin

Ariel Halliday has eight weeks to turn a darkly handsome savage into a proper gentleman. It will take a miracle . . . or maybe just falling in love.

___57520-1 $5.50/$7.50

LOVE'S A STAGE by Sharon and Tom Curtis

"Sharon and Tom's talent is immense." —LaVyrle Spencer

Frances Atherton dares to expose the plot that sent her father to prison, but soon she, too, is held captive—by the charms of London's most scandalous playwright and fascinating rake.

___56811-6 $4.99/$6.99
